GIMME SHELTER

Jack Douglas

This is the second novel by Jack Douglas who is married and has two grown up sons and lives in the Midlands. Once again, it is the coronavirus lockdown that has provided the time for him to complete this work of fiction.

Dedication
This book is dedicated to everyone who has suffered, one way or another, from the corona virus lockdowns. Hopefully it will bring a bit of light relief and escapism to a troubled world.

Acknowledgements
I would like to express my appreciation to the following people who assisted me in writing of this book;
My wife Susan for all her help
My sons David and Alan for their encouragement
Also I would like to thank my lifelong friend Gary Armstrong for all his valuable help and suggestions
Thank you to you all.
JD

PREFACE

Charlie Cooper has it all; beautiful and rich girlfriend, a top job at a leading company and all the trappings of wealth that go with his lavish lifestyle. He is an ambitious and ruthless individual who has few, if any, friends and who is full of his own self-importance to the point of arrogance.

They say that pride comes before a fall and with Charlie what a spectacular fall it is. Not only does he lose everything including his girlfriend and house, he is also accused of embezzlement, fraud and generally misbehaving.

Having been declared bankrupt Charlie meets up with Denis Jackson (aka Stringer) who helps him to adjust to his new-found poverty. Denis teaches Charlie about homeless survival and how to use some street-smart ideas to make a comeback.

Gimme Shelter is about life's ups and downs. A rags to riches story that shows how homeless people get by and the financial wheeler dealing wrongdoings that can corrupt even the best of intentions.

Does a leopard ever change its spots or is one destined to repeat the mistakes made over and over again? This and the question of morals, ethics and the consequences of a get rich quick society impact the pair and the witty and funny debates continue about the philosophy of business and the responsibilities entailed when they start to become seriously wealthy again.

Will this experience change Charlie and what will Denis do to try and keep him on the straight and narrow?

CHAPTER 1
In the beginning

"Got a cigarette?" said Charlie.

"Do I look like I can afford to give you a cigarette?" replied the tramp.

The tramp looked a bit rough sitting on the park bench like that but Charlie had just lost the lot – great job, gorgeous girlfriend, big house – everything in fact, and so what did it matter if he was bumming a smoke off a tramp.

"Here," said the tramp, "looks to me like you could do with it more than me."

"Thanks, you wouldn't believe the day I'm having," Charlie had just been declared bankrupt, homeless and generally very undesirable by a whole bunch of people some of whom he thought were his friends. He said, "I've got exactly 42p which had slipped down the lining in my jacket which I hadn't noticed and that's it. The sum total of what I'm worth."

"Day you're having is it? You want to try my life!" said the tramp, "anyway all those things you can do without. People are worth more than the money in their pocket I've usually found. Least ways the ones that matter."

So this is what it's come to thought Charlie. This time last year he reminisced that he had a big expensive car, an even bigger and more expensive house, girlfriend/fiancée and what he thought of as friends and associates. How could it all have been lost so easily and so quickly in such a short space of time?

As Charlie thought back he saw the tramp looking at him and muttering "arsehole" under his breath but Charlie couldn't help wallowing in self-pity and he felt like crying. The first time since he was about ten. It all seemed so unfair. He worked hard, done all the right things. Well, at least, what he thought was right, which admittedly was perhaps not always 'right' in a more conventional, legal or moral sense.

It was coming up to Monday lunchtime, the last week in November, and as Charlie sat there smoking with the tramp he assessed his situation and suddenly realised just how hopeless it all was. He'd had nothing to eat for over 24 hours now and was ravenously hungry. He was naturally a slim bloke anyway and because he was fairly tall looked positively skinny most of the time.

The shock of what happened was almost tipping him over the edge from a coherency point of view and on top of all that he'd got a few coins in his pocket and was trying to hold a serious conversation with what looked like an alcoholic, homeless, tramp, who seemed to be starting to actually make sense to him. The tramp was scruffy and dirty and probably aged anywhere between forty and sixty years old. It was difficult to tell under all the scruffiness.

Then it started to rain! Not just a slight drizzle but absolute buckets. Within moments the cigarettes had been extinguished and both the tramp and Charlie were very wet and very cold indeed. Oh joy thought Charlie ironically; it just keeps getting better and better.

At that point Charlie thought about ending it all, but he quickly realised that on refection he was far too important a person to contemplate such a thing. No it was all 'their' fault. The do-gooding, back-stabbers who thought they were doing society a favour by getting him the sack. Him! Who made and sold businesses, hired and fired hundreds of people and, on the whole anyway, greatly improved the general economic wellbeing of the entire country no less.

No he should be getting a knighthood not sitting here getting soaked talking to a tramp. He couldn't give up just like that though and, anyway, it would be tantamount to admitting 'they' were right and he was wrong.

He was suddenly pulled by the arm as the tramp said "We'd better get out of this rain, arsehole." The tramp tied the string holding his tatty overcoat tighter around him and pulled up the collar as the wind increased and the rain continued to pour down.

"Stop keep calling me arsehole," said Charlie, "my name is Charles Cooper or CC for short. People used to like that, the CC bit, because they said it was like yes, yes in Spanish. You know Si, Si?"

"OK arsehole, I'll make a deal with you. You stop talking like a prat and I'll call you Charlie. OK Charlie boy?"

"Charlie Boy, Charlie Boy. Where do you think you are down the East End or something? Anyway what do I call you?"

"My name's Strin... just call me Denis," said the tramp.

"OK Den where we going?" said Charlie.

"It's Denis, prat face, if you want me to call you Charlie, you call me Denis, got it? Now, just follow me and whatever happens let me do the talking and can you stop looking so posh. You don't look like you need any help and so people don't won't to help you do they? You ought to trade in your coat and get something more suitable for the streets, like me," said Denis.

"More suitable! Are you out of your mind? How am I going to make a comeback looking like a tramp? Oh no offence meant Den."

"Comeback, comeback. You ain't got a snowball in hell's chance of making a comeback. Not only ain't you got nothing but you got no chance of getting nothing either." Said Denis.

"Anything," said Charlie, "you mean anything not nothing. Two negatives make a positive."

"There you go again being a prat. You got to try and fit in more if you're going to get by 'on the road' so to speak."

Charlie, becoming somewhat exasperated said, "but I don't want to fit in, I want to get back to how things were."

"The sooner you start trying to fit in and the sooner you forget the past the better you'll be, believe you me. Drinking helps but you ain't got no money for that and so that's no good. First thing we got to do is get out of this sodding rain and get something to eat. My stomach thinks me throats been cut." said Denis.

Charming thought Charlie, but he kept his mouth shut. The tramp, Denis, Den or whatever he called himself, was right about getting out of the rain and getting something to eat though.

"So where do all good men about town or, whatever is it that you are called these days, tramps, homeless, beggars, go to then Den," said Charlie.

"We're called many things most of which ain't too polite and I'm called Denis and not Den! Probably the most common names are 'wanderers', 'drifters' or 'hitchhikers'. Some people calls us 'vagrants' or 'bums' or just swear at us. A lot don't understand. They think we do this out of choice and that really we're a load of layabouts and villains."

"Wanderer sounds OK. I'm still wondering what's actually happened to me I don't think it's really sunk in yet. But I'm going to show all those bastards when I make my comeback," said Charlie.

"In the meantime," sighed Denis, "do you have anything else other than the clothes you're in and 42p?"

"That's about it for now, but it won't be for long though, so let's just get somewhere dry and something to eat and I'll square it with you when I come back into some money."

"Oh I ain't paying," said Denis, "do you think I'd have money sitting there on that park bench looking like this? We're going for handouts at the Sally-Ann."

"Who's Sally-Ann when she's at home?" said Charlie.

"Don't you know nothing? Sally-Ann ain't a person, it's the name everyone gives the Salvation Army of course! They use a church hall not far from here which the local vicar lets them use as a type of hostel sort of thing. You can usually get a hot meal and if they ain't too full a bed for the night." said Denis rather proudly as though he'd set the whole thing up.

"A bed for the night. It don't sound too inviting," said Charlie, feeling a bit apprehensive about eating and sleeping in a church hall.

"Well unless you can come up with some readies that's the best you'll do and you want to think yourself lucky, you do, 'cos there ain't too many of these places about despite there being well over thousands and thousands of homeless people just in England alone, and most of them are actually sleeping rough on the streets night after night in all weathers. The Shelter, as it's called, only offers one night at a time, so's you can't go back there for a week or so after, so's to give everyone a chance like," explained Denis.

But all Charlie had got was the clothes on his back and 42p. What else could he do? The bankruptcy court had been bastards he thought – they'd taken everything – house, cash, credit cards, bank accounts – in fact, Charlie thought, "my entire wallet and all of my assets, such as they were these days, including my Rolex watch."

The fact that Charlie was out of work, out of accommodation and generally out of favour with just about everything and everybody. It didn't help his case of course that he had no way of repaying the large amount of debt he'd accumulated. Charlie felt that he now really knew what 'down and out' meant. Well he might be down but he wasn't out, not by along chalk he thought to himself and one of the most popular movie phrases came to him "I'll be back," he muttered, "I'll definitely be back."

Denis was looking at Charlie in a funny sort of way as though he'd seen this type of thing before. Charlie said "have you seen this type of thing before?" Denis looked a bit puzzled so Charlie elaborated, "newly bankrupted individuals!"

"Yeah, I've seen it before especially the muttering that you've started doing. That's a sure sign, the talking to yourself, that is," said Dennis.

"I was not talking to myself. I was merely remonstrating, under my breath, at the unfairness and small mindedness of certain individuals that have done this to me," declared Charlie.

"Yep, that bitter and twisted way of rationalising, and, that it's all other people who have done this to you. A sure sign all right," replied Dennis.

"A sure sign of what," said Charlie frustrated.

"A sure sign that reality ain't caught up with you yet. It don't matter whose fault it is see 'cos you're here in this mess now and there ain't no way out but you can't see that and you certainly ain't accepting it by the sound of you," said Dennis.

"No I damn well do not accept it! I made it big before and I can do it again," Charlie said confidently.

"Sure, sure," said Denis, "whatever you say," as he waved his arm to indicate the way to the church hall.

Denis carried on walking at a fairly brisk pace and Charlie had to get a move on just to try and keep up with him. Although Dennis didn't look it, he seemed to be remarkably fit for someone who was homeless and the wrong side of fifty by the look of him.

After about half hour they arrived at a fairly dilapidated church hall/mission hut. In Charlie's view it could really only be described as a hut and he immediately christened it Stalag 17 in his mind. He was just about to say to Denis it reminded him of a throwback to bygone days when Denis said, "let me do all the talking. Do not say anything to anybody in there at all. Is that clear?"

"Yeah OK. I'm hardly likely to want to socialise with these people am I?" said Charlie.

Denis just glared at him and led the way into the hall/hut which was attached to another sort of church hall which in turn was attached to a very old looking church building. Probably built in the days when this district had been a village in its own right before being absorbed into the every growing city conurbation that it now was thought Charlie.

Denis said to Charlie, "for a down and out yourself you still have quite an attitude."

"What's that supposed to mean?" said Charlie.

"Well, you come here all 'igh and mighty, but basically you sound like a bit of tosser to me."

"What do you mean by that? My circumstances are more to do with just a stupid little misunderstanding that's all. It got taken out of all proportions by a bunch of bleedin' heart do-gooders. I've worked damned hard for everything I've ever had and those bastards have took it all away."

"Yeah but if you weren't such a fly by night crook in the first place they wouldn't have taken it offa ya would they?"

"I couldn't pay my debts, that's all," said Charlie stopping at the entrance, "happens to the best of us.

"Ah but why couldn't you? No people like you only make it on the backs of others," said Denis.

"Oh please, spare me the 'unacceptable face of capitalism' speech. We live in a free society and people are free to choose what they spend their money on. So don't come bleating to me about how badly they've been treated. They go into these things with their eyes open. Caveat Emptor and all that."

"My, my I seem to have hit a bit of a nerve there haven't I?" said Denis with an amused smile on his face.

"Are we going in or what?" asked Charlie, "I'm soaked and I need to dry out a bit and I could eat a horse."

"Yes in we go and you may have to, eat a horse I mean, I'm never too sure where they get their supplies from these days with money being so tight."

Charlie said, "so how long you been sleeping rough?"

"A few years now," Denis mumbled.

"Well you ain't very good at it are you," said Charlie, "if this is the best you can come up with."

They were looking in at the church hut, which was called the Shelter, where there was a long serving table at one end with tables and chairs laid out at which sat a couple of dozen, mostly unshaven and unkempt men of a certain age, who all looked decidedly rough to Charlie. At one side of the hall were some easy to assemble units which Denis explained folded out into beds. There was a communal bathroom, but separate for men and women (not that there were many women about in general but, you never knew, just in case) in the corridor they were in, and Denis explained that they might just get a hot meal and a night's accommodation if they were lucky.

CHAPTER 2
One Year Earlier

Charlie thought back to one year ago in the offices of FinCo Plc. Was it really only 12 short months ago that things had been so different then he thought. FinCo, one of the biggest financial services, specialist firms in the business and Charlie was right up there at the top of the pile. He had worked for them for almost 10 years at that stage and he had climbed over a few 'dead bodies' at every stage of the slippery slope as they say.

It was said that Charlie had not only climbed over a few 'dead bodies' to get to the top but also 'live ones' as well and he supposedly knew where all the 'skeletons' were buried. This was very useful to Charlie because he had no qualms about blackmailing others to get what he wanted. To say he was ruthless was an understatement and he was often compared to Attila the Hun in his dealings with people.

He joined FinCo a year or so after university gaining a first-class economic degree and then a professional qualification. He worked hard and even he conceded that he'd not always played by the rules and some of the antics he'd employed had come back to 'bite' him and in a big way. He'd sailed so close to the wind that he was almost underwater but he had got results and so the company turned a blind eye to his more dodgy dealings.

He drifted back to that fateful day in Sir James Cavendish's office;

"So which one are we going for?" said Sir James Cavendish the Chairman and Chief Executive Officer, or CEO as some firms like to say, of FinCo Plc.

FinCo was an enormously successful combination of commercial banking, financial and insurance services and specialised in hedge fund type investment 'opportunities'. It was attracting funds into their company's investments that Charlie was responsible for and, once having got the funds there, he was to turn a tidy profit by investing in what is known as high yielding assets. In other words very risky investments which could wipe out entire fortunes if the firm didn't know what it was dealing with.

Charlie came up with a number of schemes over the years initially devising ways to select investment schemes that dealt with the psychology of value for money. This was what he initially termed the 'magic rule of three'. A supposedly reasonable way as the basis for a selection of choosing from several investment schemes. There would be a cheap one, a slightly more expensive 'middle of the road' type scheme and then a 'blockbuster' very costly, premium investment scheme that was the preserve of the very wealthy or those aspiring to be so.

When confronted with the 'magic rule of three' most of FinCo's clients invariably selected the middle one on the basis of being 'just right' for their needs. When the investment fund performed in a mediocre way Charlie would always inform them that it was their choice and that they had made the selection and that therefore the underperformance rested entirely with them. It was always a good ruse for those pension funds that invested with FinCo to say that it was in actual fact the funds clients' fault as they were all now living far too long for meaningful investment opportunities to take place.

No one really understood this but Charlie said it with such conviction that everyone; clients, FinCo management and employees, all went along with it. So Charlie prospered on the backs of failing investment schemes for which he could blithely say that it was others fault the investment schemes were not delivering what they promised.

Charlie then had the not so bright idea of taking this a stage further by creating a dozen new schemes at the beginning of one year, initially using FinCo's own money. He came up with all sorts of names for these; Emerging Markets, Premium Investments, Best Industrial and so on. The names meant very little as Charlie selected the stocks and shares and other investment products which went into each scheme. He devised investment schemes based on exchange traded funds which basically meant firms trading a bundle of stocks and shares whose underlying value may not be too good. At the end of that year Charlie looked at the top scheme and documented the double-digit growth in the investment funding. This was then used as marketing back up to launch future schemes on unsuspecting clients.

The fact that the rest of the schemes had either made little or, in most cases, had actually lost considerable amounts didn't faze Charlie at all. After all what he was saying about this was scheme was perfectly true and, of course, as the small print always says 'investments can go down as well as up and past performance isn't always an indicator of future performance'.

On that fateful day just over a year ago, Charlie had said to Sir James that, out of the dozen funds he had been experimenting with, the premium product one was yielding the most and so he said;

"I'm going to call it PIP! This stands for Premium Investment Product," he said proudly, "it can't fail to attract investment funds because the last 12 months have shown the value of the selected investment rising by almost 50%. I mean who's going to be able to resist such returns?"

"You're not being overly optimistic about this are you?" asked Sir James who didn't really like Charlie all that much but he tolerated his crass, money grubbing attitude because it was good for FinCo's balance sheet. Sir Charles had been Chairman and CEO of FinCo for several years and would be retiring from these positions within the next 18 months and so he wanted to go out in 'a blaze of glory' so to speak. Sir James had made a significant impact on the share price of FinCo by employing 'such smooth young fascists' as Charlie, as he liked to call them, with their totally mercenary ways and also their complete lack of moral scruples. Sir James could always take the moral high ground and, as had proved necessary in the past, distance himself if it all hit the fan and so keep his reputation untarnished.

Sir James said, "well OK then, I suppose you know what you are doing. You have full responsibility for this and it should significantly affect your targets and bonus for this coming year and so I'll leave it in your hands."

Charlie said, "no problem, this time next year I shall be picking up mega bonuses for this lot just you wait and see!" If only Charlie had realised that what he was planning was, in effect, the beginning of the end of his career, his position and his wealth.

It wasn't that Charlie was naïve but some would say that he was so 'full of himself' that he just couldn't or wouldn't see any repercussions for him or the firm. He fully believed that money could buy anything including the best legal representation you needed to get away with most things.

So Charlie launched his most ambitious investment scheme yet amidst a blaze of publicity. The returns over the past 12 months were well documented and spoke for themselves and therefore this scheme called PIP (Premium Investment Product) attracted millions and millions of pounds worth of investment from pension funds, insurance companies and banks and other financial services companies. Everyone thought it was a 'winner' and, of course, no one could have possibly believed it could fail. After all, look at the research carried out and the unique results of the preceeding 12 months performance and, of course, greed took over as well.

Initially all went well and Charlie revelled in the accolades that FinCo piled on him. He was promoted to a main board director. This meant a lot more money for him as well as share options, a top of the range Bentley motor car and the status that his ego so desperately needed.

It also enabled Charlie to propose to his girlfriend Celeste St John Smythe. Celeste was a social butterfly. She had grown up in a very wealthy part of the Home Counties, daddy was a stock-broker and mommy was 'old money' and so Celeste had never really done anything in her life. Being tall, she had tried a bit of modelling but found it all too tiresome. Charlie remembered that time 12 months ago, so clearly, when everything seemed so good. His fiancée was very pretty and whilst it wasn't exactly love at first sight he felt sure that they'd be able to make a go of it at least at the right social level. She, Celeste, hung on every word he said or so he thought. She, in actual fact, thought Char-lie was a bit rough and a bit of a social climber but because he showered her with gifts and had so much money to throw about she overlooked the rather common aspects of his behaviour and how he spoke sometimes. Charlie was tall and handsome and looked the part of a rich aristocrat and so this suited her.

She had attended a finishing school in Switzerland instead of university here in the UK and had a series of flings. At one time it was rumoured that she was dating a royal prince but it was only a rumour. However to Charlie she was the perfect mate for him and he thought he loved her. Thought because Charlie really was more in love with himself and so there wasn't a fat lot left after that to share around with other people. Charlie's narcissism was so well known at FinCo that people used to say that some people think they are infatuated with themselves but in Char-lie's case it was the real thing.

Once PIP had taken off Charlie and Celeste set the date for the wedding and bought a mansion within easy commute of the City. Although there was no real need for FinCo to be based in the City of London, Sir James and indeed most of the board of directors were traditionalists and thought that they could really only do their jobs properly within the 'Square Mile'.

This suited Charlie who reasoned that financial services companies had been robbing people for generations within the city and he thought that was a fine tradition to uphold. Charlie subscribed to the 'never give a sucker an even break' philosophy of business.

Charlie had attempted to be known as Charles in those days when he was on the way up as he was looking at the really big time and a well-bred name was really required. Well a replacement for Sir James would be needed and he was sure the old boy would recommend him after his PIP scheme had made a mountain of money.

Working all sorts of hours Charlie knew this is what he was put on this Earth to do – make more and more money and then some.

OK, so he cut a few corners here, ignored a bit of regulation there. What difference did it make everyone is on the same wavelength – everyone wants to make money and lots of it.

Charlie was very proud of the fact that he considered that his work output was 110% and whenever possible he would let people know that he was "giving it 110%" – whatever 'it' was.

Charlie never really had any close friends and those associates who he was friendly with in particular started to drift away when he was working every day – no weekends for Charles. Charlie also was very one dimensional he could only talk about his work and of course money.

And the money did come – the cars, the city apartments and all the trappings that go with it. Yeah Charles was living the dream OK but at what a price?

Charles Cooper was known as CC but pronounced Si Si according to his work colleagues because he was the ultimate 'yes Man' in the sense that none of his subordinates would say no to him. Although Charlie believed that the Si Si was because he could get things done. In reality it was a disparaging term because most of the employees at FinCo disliked and feared him.

It was said of Charles, or Charlie as he became to be known, not realising that many people used in the context of a 'proper Charlie', that he was so ruthlessly ambitious that he would literally sell his own grandmother if he could get a good price for her.

So Charlie was reliving the dream life he had such a short time ago. He had a smile on his face and his daydream was so vivid that he forgot, for a second or two, where he was now.

CHAPTER 3
Back to Reality

Charlie was brought back to the present by a torrent of abuse from Denis.

"Didn't you hear what I'm telling you, you stupid pillock!" Denis shouted.

Charlie groaned and swiftly forgot his daydream about how things had been and was rudely brought up to date with his dire predicament by Denis.

"Now listen up you ponce," Denis was saying, "otherwise you'll never get in. You look too posh and too 'igh and mighty as it is."

Charlie said, "it's only a soup kitchen, for God's sake, not the bleedin' Savoy."

"Oh so you'll be dining at the Savoy then tonight will you ….you…. you..stuck up twat!" shouted Denis.

"Well yes if I had the cash, I would," proclaimed Charlie.

"But how much cash have you got on you? You pillock!"

"Just the 42p you know – I told you – it had fallen down the lining of my jacket – I'll have to get that repaired," added Charlie absently.

"You haven't a clue what sort of mess you're in have you?" declared Denis. "No one will want to know you. People you thought of as friends will rather cross the street than talk to you. This isn't just a little embarrassment you know - this is you finished mate, washed up. You might not starve to death but you'll have to eat what you can get when you can. You have to be street smart or you could end up in the nick – mind you that's how some of them get a decent meal these days, by getting arrested."

Denis paused to take a breath and the continued, "I've been doing this for a few years now and believe you me it's no picnic and to think I used to have it all – bit like you really. Now it's a question of survival. It might not seem like it but that's what it is alright – survival and no mistake."

Charlie was sure Denis had never been like him and replied, "I'm sure it's not as bad as you make out. You seem like a fairly capable chap. Why don't you get a job and get somewhere to live? That's what I shall do. Pick myself up and start all over again."

Denis sighed with exasperation, "don't you think I've tried that? I've tried time and again to get off the streets. You go for a job and the first thing they ask (after they've guessed how old you are) is what have you been doing for the last few months. You, of course, say's out of work and you look a bit scruffy like and getting on a bit and so you've got more chance of flying to the moon than getting a job in this country. 'Land of opportunity' they say, what bleedin opportunity for people like me?"

Charlie was sure Denis was exaggerating and so he just shrugged and carried on into the makeshift hall that acted as a type of homeless hostel.

As they went through the doors the first thing that hit them was the smell. Not so much because of the unwashed stench of lots of people but more so because of that smell of desperation. Charlie had never experienced anything quite like it before.

Denis said, "you'll get used to it. It's always busy here on a Monday 'cos during the week-ends the homeless can get good pickings elsewhere. For down and outs, or wanderers, as you was calling them, that is. More likely to get a bit of change given yer or perhaps a food handout during the week-end when there's plenty of people going backwards and forwards to do a bit shopping or on a night out."

"All right Stringer!" Charlie heard one of the people queuing at the counter call out. Charlie turned his said to see who was being called but he couldn't see who it was.

"I won't be staying that long. I shall be making a start back to get on my feet by next Monday, you'll see," Charlie was saying.

Denis just shook his head and with a sad smile said, "that's what I said the first time I came here. A week's not only a long time in politics, it seems to go on forever when you're down and out."

Just then a rather jovial vicar pounced on them and said to Charlie, "thank you for bringing Denis back to us we are always worried about him now that he's getting on a bit."

"Cheeky bleeder," said Denis.

"Call me Tom," said the vicar, "my name is actually Thomas Jones but you can't believe the stick I get about that."

"It's not unusual," Charlie added without thinking.

Tom grimaced and went on to say that they had not seen Denis for a few weeks and were worried about him and so had mistakenly assumed that Charlie had brought him back to the Shelter.

"That's what we call our little offering here, a Shelter. Away from the stresses and strains of everyday life where the homeless and the lost, the wanderers as we say, can get something hot to eat and a place to sleep for the night. We're always looking out for volunteers to help and perhaps you er...Mr ..er.... might be willing to....?"

Charlie was unsure what to say and just shrugged whilst the vicar proceeded to say how worthwhile it was volunteering to work at the Shelter and that failing that any donations would be gratefully received.

At this point Charlie really felt that he should say that he had recently joined the ranks of the homeless and the lost and was just about to say so when Denis jumped in with, "'e's one of us 'e is. 'E might look like a bit of a toff but he's got nowt. Nothing at all. In fact he lost the lot today he was saying."

"Well," said Charlie, "that's not strictly true. I'd lost most of my wealth and possessions some time ago and have been living on credit ever since hoping that something will turn up. You know how it is."

"I don't really," said Tom, "I came here after reading theology at Cambridge. I felt it was where I was needed most and I can tell you I wasn't wrong there."

"Isn't there any chance of you recovering something that you would be able to live on?" Tom said to Charlie.

Charlie shook his head but said, "No Padre, but I'll be back in the high life, you watch. I'll definitely be back. They don't know who they were messing with when they turned on me." Charlie thought he may have heard these lines in a film but didn't care as they seemed to sum up his current mood.

"Who are you talking about? Who has done this thing to you?" asked Tom.

Denis just rolled his eyes and kept looking towards the hot food being served up. If they didn't hurry most of the good stuff will be gone and so he shuffled about a bit and coughed.

But Charlie was in full flow now, "Those bastards, oh excuse my French, Padre, those people at FinCo. I've given the best years of my life to that business and what do they do, the bastards. They kick me out over a few little indiscretions I ask you. As if others hadn't done worse things than that in the past. I mean we all bend the rules from time to time don't we?"

"What did you do?" said Thomas and Denis together.

"Well, I foreclosed on several loans, dismissed half of an operating department and might have, inadvertently you understand, might have taken a bit too much bonus before the board had actually sanctioned it. It was due to those penny pinching, small minded b…b….b…individuals that said that I was basically incompetent and that I had stolen the money and acted without any scruples or morals. Me! How dare they and I'd just ordered a brand-new Rolls Royce. The bastards!"

"It does rather seem harsh," said Tom.

"Harsh my elbow," said Denis, "'is 'ad 'is 'ands in the till and no mistake. You infantile git and I thought you'd just had a bit of bad luck and fallen onto hard times. You're nothing but a 'toe rag' and a crook. Worse than me. At least I was an honest worker who was 'let go' as they say for legitimate reasons. I hadn't cheated and swindled like you!"

Charlie held up his hand to placate Denis and Tom who was looking aghast at him, "I have always acted in the best interest of that firm. I have taken some very unpopular decisions and ..."

"I bet you have –sacking people right, left and centre like that – that's what happened to me that is –let go they said," said Denis.

Tom said, "well let's hope that that's all water under the bridge now shall we. Come and have something to eat and then we can talk some more afterwards."

Tom added quietly to Charlie, "sorry about that old chap. I didn't realise that you had also fallen on hard times like Denis."

"I'm nothing like Denis," protested Charlie.

"Well I'm sure that Denis will show you the ropes. He did used to be just like you, you know, and if I were you I would listen to him so that you don't end up on the streets for years on end."

Charlie shook his head laughing, "listen to that old loser? You've got to be joking. No, I'll be OK. I just need a bit of working capital and I'll be right back at the top again where I belong. You couldn't see your way clear to providing some seed capital for me to invest would you Padre? I've some great investment schemes lined up that would be right up your street."

Tom said, "Please don't keep calling me Padre, I'm not a Padre. Just a plain old vicar, perhaps priest if it sounds better. But really I have no money to invest and I make it a policy not to lend any of our 'guests' money. I barely have enough to keep going myself and as for running this place without the Salvation Army, and other charitable donations, I couldn't do it. Sorry."

Charlie was mildly disappointed, "well it's your loss Padre. My schemes are renowned for making people...."

"Redundant! Bankrupt! Suicidal?" interrupted Denis.

"I was about to say, 'comfortable, making people very comfortable'. Of course some of the great unwashed don't understand finance and so they..."

"Can be fleeced," said Denis.

Charlie gave an exasperated sigh and said, "they don't always maximise their opportunities. You must know the old saying that 'you can lead a horse to water' etc. Well some people don't seem to understand the terrific advantages of my investment schemes and admittedly some have, very occasionally lost money but the problem is they don't see the bigger picture."

"Bigger picture my arse," said Denis, "you're an out and out con man you are. You take peoples 'hard earned' and when they complain about you losing it you force them into bankruptcy. It used to be called the unacceptable face of capitalism now it seems that anything goes judging by the fall out over the last few years. You lot have got away with murder. None of you went to jail which would have been the best place for you and all you have to say for yourselves is it's all our fault because we're now living too long or we don't understand finance. The chickens have definitely come home to roost haven't they?"

"I think you are getting me mixed up with the usual run of the mill bankers," said Charlie with disdain.

"I think that's the sort of name I'm looking for," said Denis looking Charlie in the eye "banker."

They both stared at each other until Charlie looked away and said, "well let's eat. I'm starving."

Denis just shook his head and muttered something under his breath that sounded like "arsehole."

As they approached the serving counter a rather plump, middle aged lady, in a Salvation Army uniform, called out what was on offer. Charlie didn't quite catch what she said but Denis said that it was either one sort of stew or another sort of stew.

"One's for vegetarians," she said proudly.

"Do you get many vegetarians in here?" asked Charlie.

"No, I can't remember the last time we had any vegetarians. Tom can you remember the last time we had a vegetarian in here?" she shouted out.

Tom just shook his head and Charlie said, "but why do you offer a vegetarian option if there are no vegetarians?"

"Well we can't discriminate can we now?" she said. "I think it's something to do with the Human Rights thing or a left over from the EU or something or other and we've just kept on providing it."

"What happens to the vegetarian food when no one eats it?" said Charlie.

"Oh it gets eaten alright. Once the main food is gone then latecomers have the vegetarian food because that's all that's left," she replied.

"Well I think I'd like the main stew then," said Charlie.

"Oh, sorry dear, I've just given the last lot to that gentlemen over there," she said, indicating the scruffiest tramp in the place. The tramp smiled with a mouth full of food but with no teeth and which wasn't the most appealing sight Charlie had ever seen.

It wasn't enough to put Charlie off though and so he reluctantly said, "well we'd better have the vegetarian option then."

"Good choice dear. Sorry there's no bread or potatoes left but this is a turnip and swede stew and I'm sure it'll do you good. Full of nourishment I shouldn't wonder," said the serving lady.

Charlie and Denis took the stew and sat down at one of the tables to eat. Charlie tasted it and nearly gagged. He said, "it's obviously got to be good for you because it tastes so bloody awful."

Meanwhile Tom started to drift away and make his rounds amongst the other 'guests' enquiring after their health and well-being.

"I don't know," said Denis, "it's got a certain something and after a while you can't really taste much anyway. I've had worse."

Charlie tried the stew again and reluctantly pushed his plate away. "You not eating that?" said Denis looking at it keenly.

"Go on," said Charlie, "knock yourself out - you might as well have it."

CHAPTER 4
How it was, revisited

Charlie watched as Denis tucked into the stew as though it was a five star gourmet meal. Remembering just then about an earlier time, Charlie recalled when Sir James had said, "another bumper year and your bonuses will be significant."

"Yes, I'm very pleased, I've got my eye on a new car and might even go a bit further up market for accommodation," replied Charlie.

"You already have a place worth millions and that Aston Martin you insist on coming to work in each day is only 2 months old," said Sir James. "You've also got the Bentley to run around in."

"I know but I tire of these things. I mean what's the point in having all this cash if you can't do something with it?" Charlie replied.

"I know you are only relatively young – what are you now 36, 37?"

"I shall be thirty six in a few days' time and that's why I shall splash out," Charlie said with pride.

Sir James just shook his head and said, "don't you think you should provide for the future. It seems to me that however much you earn you just increase your level of spending and borrow even more always to finance a lifestyle way above your level of income. Don't you think you should start living within your means?"

"Living within my means isn't living," replied Charlie rather arrogantly. "It makes sound financial sense to borrow more now, property prices are picking up and the banks seem happy enough to lend to me. In fact, in London, property never really suffered any reductions like the rest of the country did in the latest recession. Prices may have stalled a bit but now they are back as though they've never been away. In fact I think good times are just around the corner again."

"You ever hear the saying 'Never a borrower or a lender be', Shakespeare I think, and it's what I've always strived for," said Sir James.

Charlie dismissed this and said that Sir James was just too cautious. To really benefit these days you needed to leverage up your position. He thought Sir James was starting to show his age. "Silly old sod" he thought, "he can't cut it anymore."

Sir James hated this American macho talk and pointed out to Charlie that there are people who cannot meet their obligations because of over borrowing. Sir James was saying, "It isn't very pleasant at all you know. It's typical of both businesses and individuals overstretching themselves. To paraphrase a famous financial guru 'no one should really need debt, but if you do need it, then you are probably too stupid to use it', which I think aptly describes many people these days."

In fact Sir James pointed out that the 'greed is good' mantra of the 1980's never really went away and that they were reaping the repercussions of such a disastrous philosophy even now after all these years.

Charlie was at a loss to see what Sir James was getting at. He could see nothing wrong with maximum leverage which is just a polite way of saying 'up to their necks in debt'. He said, "I think it's getting better these days but it's not as good as it once was. I do miss that sort of 'cut and thrust' and the 'survival of the fittest' that I've read about and when I was at school the 'Wall Street' video was my favourite film. Those people you talk about, Sir James, are just losers. They have no idea how they got into the state they are in. Once we get them hooked they are mine for the taking and I literally bleed them dry," said Charlie rather proudly.

Sir James thought that society had somehow missed the point. There were certainly enough resources to go round but distortions occurred because of greed and impatience. A whole credit industry had been built up on the basis of 'why wait?' This encouraged people to go into debt for instant gratification and also a way of keeping up with the Jones'. He reluctantly thought that although FinCo did need these aggressive go getters, like Charlie, and particularly since they never seemed to bother with any conscience or scruples, but God help them if anything goes wrong. He believed it was made quite clear to Charlie and those other 'free market warriors' in the firm, where they would stand and exactly what support they could expect (zero) if it all went wrong.

Charlie had later gone back to his office to study the latest car catalogues from Bentley and Rolls Royce. At his age he thought something a bit more statesmenlike is what he needed. But first he some important calls to make.

"Get me Fred Morris," he said to his long suffering secretary Penny.

She knew what was coming, poor Fred, "right away Mr Cooper," she said. Charlie didn't like any of his secretary's becoming too familiar and so he insisted on being addressed formally. His preference was for underlings to call him "sir" but he was regarded in such contempt that usually people just called him Charlie and behind his back 'a right Charlie'.

"Is that you Fred?" said Charlie.

"What do you want now?" Fred demanded.

"Well I was going to ask you to come up to my office but I think I'll let you know that I have just come from Sir James office (which was true) and we have been looking at your performance (which was untrue) and basically it's not good enough and so you're out Fred. So get your stuff together and I want you out of this building by five pm today at the latest."

"You can't do that I'm on a months' notice," said Fred.

"We are firing you for gross incompetence. Which I think you will see can be used for instant dismissal," Charlie said matter-of-factly. He knew Fred had a big mortgage and three children and wife to support but what did he care, Charlie's bonus was secured and so he carried on flicking through the car brochures as Fred ranted and raved about unfair dismissal.

"I'll go to Sir James and see what he says about this and I'll....!"

"I've just come from Sir James's office," cut in Charlie, "but by all means bother him and I think you'll see your severance cheque take a bit of a hit."

"Severance pay – what about my notice period?"

"You'll get paid in lieu if you go quietly – now I want you out and I shall be sending security to your desk at 4:30pm to make sure that you don't take any of the firm's equipment – that includes your laptop, mobile phone and company credit card."

Freed sounded utterly deflated, "but I've been with this company for almost 20 years. I've developed new products and markets and I've brought in literally millions of pounds worth of business. I just don't understand."

Charlie sounded frustrated, "there's nothing to understand – you're out and I'm in. In charge that is and so you will do as I say. Goodbye!"

Charlie sat back and thought that had gone rather well. He detested Fred. A do-gooder if ever there was one. All morals and conscience which just impeded on Charlie's business and resulted in delays and prevarication. No respect there he thought. Well his day has well and truly come.

Fred was absolutely right of course he had invented many new products and services and was really far too good to work for Charlie. He'd always tried to act in a fair and truthful manner and looked at the long-term sustainability of the business he brought in, something which was totally alien to Charlie and Charlie couldn't tolerate that sort of competitive threat from one of his staff. Sir James would understand that costs had to be cut and with Fred gone Charlie could blame Fred for a lot of the cost overruns and generally anything that he could attribute to him. A good time to wipe the slate clean with all of Charlie's misdemeanours by blaming Fred.

Charlie would subsume Fred's section under one of his other managers and generally thin out the staff a bit. He'd call it a re-organisation – should be able to get rid of at least 10% of the staff Charlie thought and that will result in another nice little bonus for me when I show how well I've managed my budgets this year. In fact not so little if all goes to plan.

Charlie continued thinking back to these type of incidents. He had been delighted when Fred had 'gone bananas' and started smashing up things. It exonerated him from any wrongdoing and blaming Fred became all too readily accepted. Charlie thought that he was very clever and could be seen with a smile on his face for the rest of that week. But on reflection now he wondered if he really should had done what he did to Fred. Was he really that insecure that he feared Fred's drive, honesty and ideas? He thought back to a year or so ago. Was it really only such a short time ago he thought when I would have had a dinner fit for a king instead of this, this … whatever this is.

It was a dinner at the Savoy he thought about. A very lavish affair. He remembered being invited to join the board at that dinner. He'd really made the big time now he thought. A forgone conclusion, of course, with his determination bordering on a ruthlessness that FinCo had never heard of let alone experienced before.

Then, it was just about a year ago Charlie realised that he'd been approached by some what he called 'do gooders' at the office where he worked. It had been a scheme to raise money for the homeless. Low cost, social housing they had called it. In fact several homeless charities had hit upon the ideas and they were to share the proceeds which would be used for further such developments. All they needed was a major backer to provide some initial funding and then, over the longer term, the schemes would virtually look after themselves.

There was virtually no risk to FinCo and it would have provided some much needed corporate social responsibility (CSR) kudos that FinCo could have used to enhance its somewhat tarnished image. FinCo, thanks to Charlie, was known as a very 'hard nosed', right wing organisation that considered free market economics 'the only game in town'. OK so individuals and organisations went to the wall- so what? Those that survived were that much stronger, weren't they? The constant fear and stress and pressure helped keep everyone on their toes especially if they had big mortgages and large amounts of debt and of course the 'system' needed them all to keep going. A constant bombardment by advertisers of the 'goodies' available if you made it – the so-called American Dream. Big house, big car, lots of gadgets, TVs, iPads etc., foreign holidays, eating out, clothes – the list goes on and on. This was the message though that is constantly dangled in front of people and if they are suckers enough to fall for it, that is that 'things' make you happy then so be it, they are fair game thought Charlie and he supposed all the other 'Charlies' in the world thought so as well.

So a good bit of CSR in the Annual Report would look really good but Charlie decided that the only money he would be interested in raising would be for himself and FinCo and he politely but firmly declined to be involved with any such schemes having such poor returns. Although he did say that the firm would continue to support whatever charity it had chosen for that particular year. Not that he knew whether FinCo did support any charity but it sounded rather good as a soundbite he thought and they could always make something up for the CSR section in the company's annual report for that year.

All that talk about homeless people had made him depressed and so he'd left work early that day to go and buy himself something expensive to cheer himself up. He planned to marry soon and his fiancée was very well connected in both the business and society worlds that Charlie firmly believed he belonged to. So Charlie thought it would be the best thing he could do to ignore any further contact with those homeless charity chappies. No, it wouldn't do his image any good at all he thought.

It was almost at that very point when his fortunes started to turn for the worse. He had overstretched himself considerably of course. He owed many millions of pounds but he had always relied on the pay rises and the bonuses. Oh those bonuses, more than most people see in their entire lifetimes in one cheque. Presented once a year around about Christmas time. Many of his colleagues rushed out to buy new cars Porsche, BMW etc. Charlie was above all that of course. He was in the Rolls Royce league now and he really needed the bonuses to pay down his and Celeste's debt. He was bad enough, but Celeste had no concept of thrift. She had been brought up always to have whatever she wanted regardless of cost and so she behaved like a spoilt child and sulked for days on end if she couldn't have the latest designer dresses by the famous fashionistas. A single dress could cost well over £20,000 and invariably would be worn once.

Charlie's PIP scheme had not been performing at all well. Charlie didn't really expect it to since he only had one year's worth of data which happened to be good. There was no reason at all why the following year should be any good. After all if was just a punt on his part, a bit of a guess as to which investments within the PIP portfolio would bring in the big returns that he had promised investors. No such returns had been received and the PIP fund stood at about half of the value invested. In other words Charlie had lost many millions of pounds of FinCo's client's money. In most cases their original investments were worth less than half their original stake once fees had been taken into account.

Charlie wasn't worried; he repaid all of FinCo's own money, which he had 'advanced' himself, once the clients investments started to roll in. A bit like a 'Ponzi Pyramid Scheme' he thought at the time. But he had took out not only FinCo's money but also some management fees, most of which he pocketed as a 'bonus advance'. This may have been acceptable if PIP had done well and if he had mentioned to Sir James that he had taken the advance. Although Charlie believed he had informed Sir James in a roundabout way. This was strenuously denied by the Chairman's office and reading between the lines Sir James had intimated that there were 'certain irregularities' which is a polite way of saying someone has had their 'hand in the till'.

If this wasn't bad enough the Financial Regular the FCA, as it was called, felt very strongly that FinCo had mis-sold PIP. They had misled their clients and the risk and return nature of the investment scheme had not been sufficiently spelt out. The fact that investors were losing money hand over fist and were very vocal about it, strengthened the FCA's resolve to bring an action against FinCo and criminal charges against Charlie for fraud on a massive scale.

This was the worst time of Charlie's life. Celeste had left him as soon as the money dried up and also the social stigma of being engaged to a crook meant that she would have nothing whatsoever to do with Charlie. This immediately cut off a large number of contacts that Charlie had used in the past for business. Also wherever he went he was pointed out and either doors were closed to him or he was asked to settle in cash, in advance. So soon he had to stop going to upmarket restaurants, hotels and his posh membership clubs and settle for eating in. This was exacerbated very quickly as the mortgage and loans he secured to buy his big house and cars were called in immediately. Of course with no bonus money and very little savings Charlie defaulted on the large amount of debt he owed.

The bankruptcy and debt collection summonses started to arrive. The FCA had issued legal actions against him one of which was a fine of one million pounds. Another was a warrant for his arrest for criminal fraud activities.

Sir James would have nothing to do with him. He automatically took Charlie's name off the circulation lists, informed all of the board to have nothing to do with Charlie and also made sure that none of Charlie's colleagues or peers would have any contact with Charlie whatsoever. Sir James pointed out that anyone associating with Charlie might be considered to be guilty by association. No one wanted to be associated with Charlie at all. He was very definitely out and on his own.

Once the fines and the repayments had been made and, of course having no job and no income, Charlie used his credit cards to book into a hotel. He had a few clothes in a bag and a few pounds in cash but basically he still owed millions, was facing trial for fraud and was a complete social outcast.

In just about 12 months he'd gone from millionaire status to flat broke and now he was down and, dare he say it? – OUT. Well and truly out by the look of his surroundings. He was lucky he hadn't been convicted and imprisoned.

CHAPTER 5
How the mighty have fallen

Suddenly Charlie was brought back to the present by a shout directed at Denis "Oi you, Stringer, are you eating two lots of the stew?" This was being shouted at him by a huge, toothless vagabond who looked at least fifty years old but was probably still in his thirties. A big, heavy bloke though so Charlie said, "I think he needs it more than you pal."

"I ain't your pal, you ponce," retorted the big bloke who scowled at Charlie as though he would really like to 'punch out his lights' as they say. He said 'what you got to give me, ponce?"

Charlie sighed and said, "I've given away my food, I've got 42p to my name, what more do you want?"

"Well, that coat you're wearing looks pretty good from where I'm sitting, I think I'll have that," the toothless wonder said, and smiled a gummy smile that would have been comical if it wasn't so menacing.

"Get stuffed!" said Charlie, "this coat cost me a bundle and there is no way you're getting it."

"Give him the coat Charlie or you wont' be able to walk out of here," said Denis.

"You keep out of this Stringer," said the toothless wonder.

"If you hadn't had all your teeth knocked out then I'd knock them out now," said Charlie. He turned to Denis and said, "who's this Stringer bloke they keep on about?"

"I'm Stringer," said Denis.

"Why do they call you that?" asked Charlie.

"Because I use string to keep my coat tied around me, like this see," said Denis indicating the string around the middle of his threadbare overcoat. "It sort of just stuck, and so everyone here, except Tom that is, calls me Stringer."

"This big bloke here who's after your coat used to be a boxer but it sent him a bit mad and so he's now called Psycho Sid. In fact most people here have got nicknames. I think that they would rather have it that way. That gentleman over there kept 'finding' brief cases and so he's called Suitcase. After a time you forget, if you ever knew, what their real names are."

Charlie looked around at the sorrowful state of the people there. Mostly older blokes who had played the game of life and lost and lost big time thought Charlie.

He was still hanging onto his coat when Denis whispered to him, "let him have the coat Charlie. The last bloke Sid tangled with is still in hospital and that was a couple of weeks ago."

"No," said Charlie, "I may have lost everything but I'm not losing the coat off my back. If this toothless wonder, Psycho Sid wants it he'll have to come and fi.... aghhh...." as Sid knocked Charlie off his feet.

Charlie went flying over the tables and chairs and ended up in a pile against the wall. Sid walked over to him and assumed a sort of boxer's stance ready for Charlie to launch an assault on him. Charlie wasn't too sure what day of the week it was let alone trying to stand up to face off against Sid. So Sid bent down and picked him up like he was a rag doll and proceeded to 'help' Charlie out of his coat. Sid put it on but it was far too small with the sleeves ending by the elbows and it looked more like a long jacket that a posh Crombie overcoat.

"Sid you look ridiculous," said Denis, "it's far too small for you. Give it back to him and say you're sorry."

"Huh," snarled Psycho Sid, "it's all his fault, the ponce. He's too short he is. As well as being a ponce," he added.

"Give him the coat back," repeated Denis thinking Charlie's no shorty but Psycho Sid is huge by comparison.

Everyone in the hall had stopped whatever they were doing and were looking at the scene being played out at the end of the hall. Charlie was holding onto a table to support himself as he was still feeling a bit groggy after the blow from Sid. Denis was holding out his hand to Psycho Sid who was still pirouetting in the coat trying to convince himself that it fitted him.

Denis looked hard at Sid and said, "come on Sid, it's no use to you, give it back."

Psycho Sid reluctantly took the coat off and threw it at Charlie who was still disoriented and so it just slid down him to the floor.

Sid stormed off back to the serving counter and asked for something to eat.

"It's all gone now dearie," said the serving lady, "that's it for today I'm afraid. You'll have to come back tomorrow."

"Tomorrow!" shouted Sid, "what am I supposed to do until then. I'm bleedin' starving, I am, and that vicar's got it in for me as well."

"Come now dear, Tom's only trying to be fair to everybody," said the cook, "you know there's never really enough to go around everybody and you knows the rule about one night a week here so's to give everyone a chance."

Charlie managed to stand up and put his coat back on noticing the split seams. He faced up to Psycho Sid who had returned from the counter and said, "that showed you," and Sid just looked at him like he couldn't believe what he was hearing and then he just laughed as he walked out of the hall shaking his head.

Just then Tom the vicar strolled up and said, "what's going on here? You finished your food already?"

"I just need to pop out for some fresh air," said Charlie, as he started after Sid looking for something heavy to hit him with.

"Oh no you don't," said Denis, "you're staying here now, and so you might as well find a bunk and start settling down for the night."

Tom said, "that's the idea, everything will look so much better in the morning after you've had a good night's sleep. Are you staying as well Denis? You've not been here for a couple of weeks?"

"If it's all right with you vicar. Yes I'd like to stay," said Denis.

"Of course," said Tom, "you're very welcome Denis, you know that. You've helped us from time to time and I know you'll help get breakfast in the morning. Perhaps Charlie could help you if he feels up to it. Mind you he looks a bit peaky at the moment."

"He'll be all right Vicar, I'll show him the ropes," said Denis.

Charlie said, "I don't know if I'm going to be able to do this Stringer, sorry Denis. I just don't think that I'll be able to stay here overnight."

"Well you got two choices," said Denis, "you can either stay here where it's dry and reasonably warm. Or you can chance your arm outside on the streets with the likes of Psycho Sid for company. Last time I looked it was still pissing down, the winds got up and it's bleedin' freezin'. But if that's what you want off you go son, you're on your own."

Charlie thought about what Denis said and it obviously made sense to stay in the church hall for that night. After all Charlie thought it's only one night and tomorrow is another day. It'll look better in the morning.

Who am I trying to kid thought Charlie as his arrogant, self-assurance left him for probably the first time in his life. Just then tears of self-pity started to well up in his eyes. He turned away from Denis and slumped down on a very small bunk bed, still fully dressed, and clutching his coat tight around him he sort of rocked backwards and forwards with a strange humming noise coming from him.

Denis said, "it will look better in the morning Charlie, you wait and see. I ain't been on the streets these past few years without learning a thing or two and I'll show you the ropes."

"Wow, ain't I the lucky one! Show me how to get breakfast for a couple of dozen bums," said Charlie, "yeah that's right bums. Who are we trying to kid? Wanderers don't cut it at all. We're just bums. Me and you and the rest of this flea bitten, mangy lot of down and outs."

Charlie gave a big sigh and shuddered whilst Denis looked at him with a degree of pity. Denis knew how rough it can be for a new person, used to having a wealthy lifestyle, to join the ranks of the homeless. He didn't think people generally gave up hope quite so quickly but then again Charlie had had a lot further to fall than most people.

Denis thought he must try and give Charlie some hope before they went to sleep otherwise if he woke during the night Charlie might do himself some harm if he thought his situation was truly hopeless.

So Denis said, "I got some great ideas on how to get back on top and all I've been waiting for is someone with a bit of go about them to help me get them off the ground. Someone like you Charlie."

"What ideas?" said Charlie, "you talking about mugging some old dears or something like that, 'cos as low as I am I ain't into any of that physical robbery stuff you know, not yet at least."

"What! You just like robbing them when they can't see you, is that it?" Denis shouted.

"I don't know what you mean," said Charlie, "I told you it's been a complete miscarriage of justice that's all."

"Of course it has," said Denis, relieved that Charlie seemed to be finding some inner strength from somewhere, "just you wait and see. I got some great ideas to get us back to where we belong."

CHAPTER 6
Tomorrow's another day

It was still dark as the commotion woke Charlie from a fitful sleep, "what the f......," he said as he spotted Tom coming towards him. "Morning vicar," he said, "what time is it?"

Tom said, "it's just about 6:00 o'clock. I thought you would want to be up early as you and Denis kindly volunteered to prepare breakfast for us all."

"Oh," said Charlie, not really remembering where he was let alone volunteering to cook breakfast for a couple of dozen people. "What do we do for breakfast then? Eggs and bacon is it?"

Tom smiled and shook his head saying, "if only we could, but I'm afraid the only things we can afford are some cereal and toast."

Just then Denis stirred, "did you sleep OK Charlie?" he asked.

"No, I bloody well didn't," said an ungrateful Charlie, "I kept falling off the bunk bed, and trying to get back to sleep with that row going on! The snoring was incredible, I mean what have these people been doing to snore like that, the tiles were rattling on the roof!"

"You'll get used to it," said Denis without thinking.

"Now Denis, you know the rules, it was just for one night until next week," said Tom.

"Oh, yeah, right, I was forgetting," replied Denis.

"Well where am I going to sleep tonight," complained Charlie.

"I think I can find a park bench with your name on it," said Denis and before Charlie could reply added, "come on let's get this breakfast sorted before they wake up and start having a go about it not being ready. They can be a nasty bunch first thing."

The kitchen, if it could be called that, looked like a throwback to the 1950's. The only 'modern' things were a six slice toaster, which had seen better days, a huge tea urn, which looked like the kitchen had been built around it because it was so big, and a vintage fridge although it was so cold in the kitchen Charlie wondered why they would want a fridge.

However, once they started toasting the catering sliced loafs and brought the urn up to boil it became as hot as an oven and, for the first time since he arrived, Charlie took off his overcoat.

Denis was putting the six slices in the toaster at a time and Charlie was buttering them as they pinged up. Quite what he was buttering them with he wasn't quite sure, it looked a bit like axle grease and melted away to nothing as soon as it was applied to the toast.

"What exactly am I buttering this toast with?" enquired Charlie.

"It's a low-fat spread of some description. Tom gets it cheap from the cash and carry wholesalers," said Denis.

"I've never seen anything like it. Are you sure it's fit for human consumption?" replied Charlie.

"You'll get to realise Charlie, that when you're hungry even the most unappetising food gets snapped up," said Denis.

"I'm not going to be around that long to find out," said Charlie, his bravado coming back. "No, I'll be moving on to try and start rebuilding my life today."

"So, how are you planning to do that then?" asked a sceptical Denis.

"Oh, I'll find a way....," Charlie was about to say more when there was an angry shout, "where's the cornflakes, look this pair haven't even put the corn flakes out yet, lazy buggers."

"Hold your hair on Digger, well what you've got left that is," said Denis, "we're just coming through now, and the toast is ready as well."

Digger wasn't impressed and said, "and the tea, don't forget the tea."

"I'd rather have coffee of a morning Denis, if it's all the same to you," Charlie said.

"No problem," said Denis, "if you can find any coffee then you're welcome to it.

Charlie looked out at all these odd men all shovelling cornflakes down as though there was no tomorrow and, he thought, I suppose for some of them there is no tomorrow. Not one worth looking forward to anyway. The noise as they ate their breakfast was deafening and Denis was saying to him, "you'd better eat something Charlie because it'll all soon be gone."

"Denis, I really don't think I could eat this shit," replied Charlie.

"Well it's your loss, you'll feel hungry later and regret not having something," said Denis.

Charlie was about to try the cornflakes when he realised that they had all gone. "Where's the rest of the cornflakes Denis?" he said.

"Oh, there's only enough for the people here this morning. The budget is very strict here and breakfast is a bowl of cornflakes and a couple of rounds of toast with a mug of tea, and that's it, I'm afraid. If you don't get in quick then your quota gets snapped up pretty quickly by the others.

"Oh well, I'll just have a cup of tea," said Charlie, "I take it there's some left in that huge urn."

"Only just," said Denis, "here I'll tip it up for you so that you get what's left at the bottom."

The tea oozed out of the urn with a consistency of custard and

Charlie wasn't sure if it was a spoon or a knife and fork he'd need to drink it with.

As there were no more cornflakes, toast or tea, the people started to file out of the hall. Picking up what personal bits and pieces they possessed they sullenly went out of the hall into the cold morning.

"Why aren't there any women in here?" asked Charlie

"Separate accommodation for the girls," Denis said, "the vicar uses a meeting room at the rectory for women."

"The dirty old sod," said Charlie.

"No it's not like that. It's the only place they are likely to be safe. Life on the streets Charlie is no 'fun and games', believe you me."

Charlie thought about what Denis was saying and said, "you don't actually see that many women on the streets do you?"

Denis said, "no, it's more common for men to fall on hard times than women. Don't really know why that is but I think most men still take on the financial responsibilities and also, perhaps, men aren't as good as they think they are at controlling money."

"Yeah," said Charlie, "I remember my hero, Maggie Thatcher, saying that we should have housewives managing the country because they know they have to manage the household expenses to keep everyone fed."

"Trust you to have Maggie Thatcher as a hero," said Denis, "anyone else it would be sport stars or celebrities of some sort or other."

"Listen, this country wouldn't be where it is today without what Maggie did in the 1980s." replied Charlie. "She was the only one to stand up to the trade unions and she brought about a revolution in financial services and generally deregulated many markets giving us all a lot more freedom."

"That's why there are still many millions of people unemployed and why over the past few decades that the homeless, of which you are now one, has increased by so much!"

"You don't understand, you moron. The markets are now much more efficient and so the economy benefits and......," Charlie was saying when Denis interrupted.

"I understand only too well you prat. The rich have got richer and the poor no longer have the safeguards they used to have. So you can be thrown out of you home more easily now for not paying your mortgage or your rent. The morals and scruples have all been swept aside for the sake of making a few quid," said Denis with feeling.

Charlie was shaking his head, "Denis, Denis, you are so old fashioned. The world has moved on since your day."

"And not for the better, I might add," replied Denis. "I think we'd better leave the argument there, otherwise I think you and I are going to fall out with one another."

"OK," said Charlie, "where are we going to go?"

CHAPTER 7
Tuesday and all's not well

Charlie and Denis walked the streets looking for some handouts and somewhere they could stay overnight. Most of the squats were taken but they came across a big old house which had recently become vacant and looked ready for demolition. "This'll do us for tonight," said Denis, "let's go to the back of that hotel in the High Street to see if we can get some handouts and then come back here before all the slots get taken."

"What do you mean 'taken'?" asked Charlie.

"Well, what you need to realise there's a certain etiquette in choosing a squat. You can't just turn up and pick any old place to doss down. Oh, no, someone might already have a claim to it and unless you want your head kicked in then you have to respect that." Denis was explaining.

Charlie was shaking his head and said, "It's only a bleedin' derelict house for heavens sake!"

Denis replied, "you've got an awful lot to learn you have. You've got to realise that the normal rules of civilisation are out of the window now and you are looking at survival. But there are a lot of other homeless people looking for survival too and so it's sometimes becomes survival of the fittest – you were into that weren't you, at one time, free market and survival of the fittest and the rest can go to the 'wall' and all that?"

"Not like this I wasn't," said Charlie despondently.

"No, it's bit different when your very existence depends on it, isn't it?" Denis said as they found a vacant upstairs room.

CHAPTER 8
What a week that was

Charlie and Denis were able to stay in the squat for most of that week and it wasn't until the Friday night that they got moved on by some workmen who were putting up no entry signs and fencing prior to demolition.

Charlie had stopped in the squat on that Tuesday whilst Denis foraged for some food behind a couple of the hotels on the main road. Usually after lunch and dinner times the leftovers, after the staff have eaten, are just thrown out. Denis had got to know some of the kitchen staff and they would give him food that they were about to throw away. It was perfectly edible but wasn't worth keeping and so it was either thrown out or given to the homeless.

So Charlie and Denis ate as good as the hotel guests on that Tuesday and although it was cold they were at least dry.

Denis said, "this is a bit of a find this is. If we can stay here for a while we'll be alright."

"I don't want to just be alright," complained Charlie, "I want to make a start on getting back on top of things."

"Oh, and how are you going to go about doing that then?" enquired Denis.

Charlie just shrugged and said that he would think of something.

They both woke with a start on the Wednesday morning as a couple of other homeless blokes were trying to get into their part of the squat. It was a bitterly cold morning being the end of November and there was ice on the windows in the room where Charlie and Denis were. Suddenly they heard someone banging on the door and the door being pushed open. Denis had put some old timber in front of the door before going to sleep to stop anyone else coming into the room.

They heard, "c'mon, open up, we're know you're in there!" being shouted from behind the door.

"What'd yer want?" said Denis.

"We want to get in, that's what we want!"

"Piss off!" shouted Charlie.

Denis thought he knew the voice and said, "why do'ya wanna get in here for?"

"Because we're freezing our bollocks off out here," said the voice.

Denis then recognised the voice and said to Charlie, "it's that Scouser from the Shelter. I think they call him Merseyside Billy."

"Who you got with you, Billy?" asked Denis

"Is that you Stringer? It's Bert the Brummie, you know him and me so let us in."

"Give us a hand to move this wood Charlie," said Denis

Charlie looked aghast and said, "you're not going to let them come in here are you?"

Denis said, "Oh, Billy and Bert are OK. I've known them for quite a while. C'mon let's get this wood shifted."

As they opened the door there stood two of the most miserable and scruffy looking men Charlie had ever seen. Both were wearing threadbare overcoats that looked to be too big on the one and too small on the other and Charlie wondered why they didn't swap them over.

Both of these new visitors looked frozen although they had scarfs and gloves and what looked like several layers of clothes on. They were hugging themselves trying to get warm and they were shivering uncontrollably.

"What's happened to you two then?" asked Denis.

Billy manged to get a few words out between his chattering teeth, "we slept rough the back of Sainsbury's last night. We'd just got a couple of cardboard boxes and the clothes we're wearing."

"That must have been rough," said Denis.

"You're telling us," said Bert in the broadest Brummie accent possible.

"How come you're down in this part of the world?" asked Charlie, "you both sound as though you're a long way from home."

Billy said, "I moved down here with my job and no soon as I was settled and with a bloody big mortgage, I can tell you, then they made me redundant. Never saw it coming and we'd used all our savings to get down here. I couldn't get another job, the debts started to pile up..... and the missus left me..... so it weren't all bad news I suppose."

Charlie couldn't tell if he was joking and so just asked what did he used to do for a living. Billy and Bert said that they'd both been working in good engineering jobs but what with recessions and with automation being installed everywhere, there was at least a couple of hundred people chasing every job that came up.

Denis sympathised but all Charlie said was that they needed to retrain and find themselves jobs in different areas.

Bert and Billy looked at him and Billy said, "we've both been doing those jobs for more years than I care to remember now and so it's going to be a bit difficult to retrain to do something else. Engineering is all we know. In any case who's going to retrain us at our age?"

Denis just shook his head and said, "how come you ended up at Sainsbury's, couldn't you find another flop anywhere?"

"Naw, we'd used up our noight at the Shelter loike, and none of the other charities had anything on offer, loike, and so we walked the streets for a bit, loike, to try and keep warm, but we were both knackered and so we needed to bed down somewhere and that was about the only place left," said Bert.

"You need to be careful at that Sainsburys you know because some of the local hooligans come round late at night and beat you up," said Denis.

Charlie looked confused and said, "you don't mean people deliberately pick on you just 'cause you're sleeping rough?"

"Too right they do," said Denis, "It's happened to me on more than one occasion I can tell you."

Billy and Bert both nodded and said that there were some big blokes who roughed them up. They wondered if they been secretly employed by Sainsbury to clear that part of the car park where the homeless slept rough. Billy went on, "they said not to go back there because next time they wouldn't be so understanding whatever that meant."

Denis said, "I think it means Sainsburys is out of bounds from now on unless you want your head kicked in."

Charlie couldn't believe what he was hearing and was sure it was all a misunderstanding.

"You and Bert kip down here then for now, while me and Charlie go and see if we can get us all something to eat. Put that wood up against the door when we've gone and only open the door for us otherwise we'll have half the homeless in here before you know it," said Denis.

CHAPTER 9
Wednesday

So Denis and Charlie set forth on that Wednesday morning in search of food. It was too early for the hotels and Denis thought they might try a bit of begging in front of one of the supermarkets. Charlie was totally against this and said that he'd rather been seen dead than beg. Denis suggested that it might well come to that if their prospects didn't look up soon.

Eventually they agreed to do a bit of shoplifting. Charlie was totally against this idea as well and Denis was trying to placate him by saying that all of the supermarkets budgets for this sort of thing and so's it's not like they're stealing but more like the cost of their purchases would be spread over a number of other people who would almost certainly give them money if they knew their predicament.

This argument confused Charlie which was a good thing and since he still looked reasonably presentable, he would be going into the shop and using the self-scan facility to buy a newspaper, a box of matches and a plastic carrier bag and then to put a load of other things in his basket which he just wouldn't scan through.

Charlie did not want to do this and Denis had to remind him how hungry he was. Not that Charlie needed reminding about the knawing hunger that always seemed to be with him these days. "But," Charlie was saying, "I don't have enough for a paper and matches. Remember I only have 42p. It's not really very credible me going in there with that amount now is it?"

Denis said, "here's a couple of pounds, and I want the change and, don't get anything in cans, nothing that needs to be cooked, nothing in any wrapping that we can't get off. Remember we've got no scissors, no tin openers, no pots or pans. So use your common sense."

Charlie reluctantly went through into the shop and Denis waited outside around the corner from the car park. It was still bitterly cold and he had to keep stamping his feet to try and keep warm.

Denis was very surprised that Charlie had managed to pull off the shopping expedition and, other than the fact that Charlie was looking round rather furtively, when he came out of the shop he'd managed to do exactly as he was told.

Denis and Charlie quickly hurried back to the squat to divide up the food with Bert and Billy.

Bert said in his broad Brummie accent, "oi doint loike pork pies and oim not too keen on sawsage rolls oither!"

Charlie just looked at him and said to Denis, "what did he say?"

"He says you done good in getting the things he likes," said Denis with his fingers crossed behind his back.

"Oh, that's alright then," said Charlie, "I thought he was having a go at what I'd managed to get."

Billy jumped in and said, "don't mind Bert, he ain't happy unless he's moaning about something. We'll all get stuck into this nosh, thanks."

In addition to the pork pies and sausage rolls, Charlie had managed to purloin some pieces of cooked chicken, some bread and some cheese. Denis had said to him that he had done remarkably well for a first timer to which Charlie had replied, "first and last time".

Bert continued, thinking aloud said, "oim not too keen on bread without butter me, loike, no I just can't eat it loike that, it's too dry."

Charlie just said, "well you can get the food in next time can't you? I dunno, one day in the squat and they're getting choosy about what they eat."

"Just like you Charlie," said Denis, "don't pretend that you didn't turn your nose up about some of the food you've had over the past few days."

"That's different because I'm still adjusting, you know, the shock and everything?" said Charlie.

Denis was saying to Billy, "it looks like we all might be OK in here for the time being. You and Bert can go and get the nosh tomorrow and me and Charlie will stay here. I think someone needs to be here all the while because there are a lot out there who'll have this from under our noses if we aren't careful."

"That's OK with us, isn't it Bert?" said Billy, "with the weather like it is at the moment we need somewhere inside that's dry. No good kipping on park benches this weather, oh, no."

"That OK with you Charlie?" asked Denis.

Charlie thought for a moment and said whatever works for the time being. He was still pondering how to get back 'into the game' as he put it.

The rest of the day was spent looking at the newspapers, the one they'd bought plus the newspaper people had recently thrown away that they'd picked up on the way back to the squat.

CHAPTER 10
Another Day, Another Dollar (if only)

Thursday started off pretty much the same as the Wednesday and Billy and Bert kept their part of the bargain and went to get the food. They thought that they would try a different supermarket today and Bert was saying he fancied some cake. Billy was saying that he would get it and Bert could wait outside. He asked if he could borrow Charlie's overcoat which looked much more presentable than his own and Charlie reluctantly agreed.

They managed to put together a couple of pounds worth of coins and off they went, leaving Charlie and Denis to guard the squat.

Billy and Bert weren't as well organised as Denis and were constantly bickering about what they were going to get. Billy was saying, "look Bert, if we try and get all that it's going to give the game away. We can only get a few things. Remember what Denis told us? Scan one then miss an item, then scan the next, then miss one."

Bert was sulking and just said, "Oh, OK then, just don't forget me cake. oim off round the corner, loike, to do a bit of begging. I might pick up something…"

"You'll pick up a cold arse, sitting on the pavement there, that's what you'll pick up," said Billy.

"We'll see then won't we," said Bert as he ambled off, in a bit of a strop, to find a spot where he could catch people's eye as they came out of the shop but not too close otherwise the shop staff would clear him off.

Billy couldn't find Bert initially, after he came out of the shop, and it was only as he walked a bit further that he saw him shivering on the pavement outside a bank. Billy went up to him and said, "have you done any good here?"

Bert said that sometimes when people come out of the bank they slipped him a few coins or the odd pound. "I reckun io've managed to get a few quid while yo been in the shop," said Bert, "what did yo manage to get then in the end loike?"

Billy said that it hadn't been easy but he got some cake, that Bert had insisted on, and some biscuits and some cold meat pies.

"Is that it?" said Bert, "that ain't gooing to keep us gooing very lung is it?"

"Well you want to try it next time," said Billy, "it's not that easy and it's a good job I'm wearing Charlie's overcoat because I was getting some funny looks from the shop assistants."

Bert said, "yo don't wanna tek no notice of them."

"D'you know Bert, sometimes I can't understand a word you say. Are you sure you're speaking English?" Billy replied.

Bert just started off back to the squat, mumbling something about Billy washing his bleedin' ears out.

At the squat, Charlie and Denis had been having a bit of a time of it as a group of young lads tried to get in to get them out. They kept shouting about the place was going to be knocked down and that if Denis and Charlie didn't leave then they would just knock the building down on top of them.

Shortly after they'd gone Billy and Bert arrived and Charlie said, "oh, that's really healthy that lot; cake, biscuits and meat pies. Talk about your 'five a day' that's nowhere in sight!"

"Bert wanted cake and the other things were all I could get quickly. I needed to be in and out quick because I thought they were going to throw me out. I know I got your overcoat on Charlie, but I still look homeless – I can't help it." Billy replied.

Denis told Billy and Bert about the hooligans trying to get into the squat and asked if they'd seen any workmen outside.

Both Bert and Billy shook their heads and said that they hadn't seen anyone outside as they came back.

Charlie said, "I wonder if they just wanted us out so that they could use this squat. What do you think Denis?"

"Well there's no point in wondering about it now. I think we're OK for another night here and then we'll just have to see what happens tomorrow." He replied.

So they ate the food that Billy had brought back. Had a look at the newspaper to see if there was any casual work they could pick up and generally chatted about what scams they had been up to. Charlie listened fascinated to Billy and Bert who sounded like a couple of rogues. Both had been on the streets for a while and done a bit of begging and a bit of thieving when they could get away with it. Denis also it seems had got his 'hands dirty' from time to time. Denis kept saying, "It's no good looking like that Charlie. You do what you need to do to survive. You can't always rely on handouts or charity from the Sally Ann."

Charlie said, "I'm not going to become a common thief, so you can forget that straightaway."

"I thought you'd be good at that with your track record," said Denis.

"I never robbed anyone!" protested Charlie.

Denis laughed, "yes you did. You think because it was done on such a large scale that it don't count. But what you did was crooked and you also ripped of the business you were working for – don't forget that."

"That was different," said Charlie, "I told you it was a bit of a misunderstanding, that's all."

"Having it away with a few million of the firms money, a bit of a misunderstanding, I don't think so," continued Denis.

"Well look at what you lot have been up to; shoplifting, begging, stealing and such like. None of you lot are whiter than white so don't lecture me on morals!" said Charlie.

"ooo...." chorused the others and Billy said, "don't throw yer toys outa the pram mate, we're only winding you up."

"Well don't!" said Charlie, "I've got enough to contend with without bantering with you lot all night."

So they settled down for another night in the squat.

CHAPTER 11
Eviction

They were all woken up early by an almighty crashing and banging. As they struggled to get up from under their coats and whatever they'd used to keep warm, it dawned on them that the hooligans from yesterday were back.

Billy and Bert were looking scared and Charlie shouted to Denis, "what are we going to do?"

Denis told them all to keep calm as he approached the door, still barricaded with the wood that they had been using to keep the door secure from outsiders. He said, "Who is it, and what do you want?"

A rough voice from the other side of the door said, "c'mon you lot, time to move on now. We told you yesterday that demolition was starting today and unless you want to be buried under a few ton of rubble you'd better get out of there now."

"Can you give us ten minutes to get our stuff together?" asked Denis.

"Ten minutes? OK, but you'd better get a move on, the wrecking ball is already here and the physcopath driving in is called Screw Lose Larry. So you'd better not keep him waiting too long because he'll start knocking the place down whilst you're all in there!"

Charlie and Billy and Bert were all hopping from foot to foot shouting, "what'll we do now? what'll we do now?"

Denis raised his hands to placate them and said, "come on, lets get what bits and pieces we have an get out of here. I don't fancy being buried under all this lot, do you?"

The others all nodded and proceeded to pick up their stuff,

which mainly consisted of clothes, and started to remove the wood from the door in order to get out.

They could hear a voice shouting, "Come on, Come on! We haven't got all day you know."

The four of them shuffled out of the room to be confronted by several very large blokes wearing fluorescent jackets, hard hats and severe frowns.

The one who had shouted through the door looked to be the foreman and he said, "come on you lot, let's be 'aving yer!"

Charlie and Denis just nodded and made their way out of the building followed by Billy and Bert. Once outside they all shivered as there was a biting wind. "Well we'll be off, been good," said Billy.

"Yeah, tar.ar.a.bit, loike," said Bert and off they went.

Charlie said, "well that's got rid of them."

"Why do you do that Charlie?" asked Denis, "you're always having a go at other people. Listen, you're no better than them and you may even be worse than them. They've at least had a bit of experience on how to survive especially when the weather's like this. I bet you don't know which way to turn now, do you?"

Charlie just shrugged and said, "I thought they were a bit rough that's all."

Denis shook his head and said, "come on, let's see if we can find something to eat from somewhere and then we need to see where we're going to kip tonight."

They both walked the streets for some time, just trying to keep warm. It was no easy task at this time of year. The people were all rushing back and forwards and tried to avoid Denis and Charlie as best they could for fear of being 'tapped up' for money. The shops were now all decorated out for the Christmas season and generally there was a very busy 'buzz' all over town.

They went to the back of the one hotels that Denis tended to go to and after the lunch crowd had dispersed the kitchen staff were about to throw out some leftovers when Denis asked if he could have them. There wasn't an awful lot of food but what there was would keep them going for a while.

They ended up walking the streets again then, after they'd had something to eat, looking for a place to bed down for the night.

In the end, that Friday night they had to sleep rough and they surveyed a few potential areas. The first one under a fly-over roadway was dry enough but very cold. What put them both off though was the noise from the cars above which was pretty constant during the day and Denis reckoned it would be just as busy at night. They looked at the back of Sainsbury's but didn't fancy that after what they'd heard about homeless people being beaten up for sleeping there. So in the end they settled for a park bench. At least the weather is a bit better this Friday night they thought although still very cold.

CHAPTER 12
The park bench

The weather was marginally better being dry but it got colder and colder during the night. "At least it's not raining," said Denis just before the heavens opened and a short sharp shower started.

"Quick, under the railway bridge," he said.

Charlie just pulled his collar up and followed him in a desultory manner under the bridge where it wasn't any warmer but it was relatively dry.

Charlie said, "I'm still bloody cold under here!"

"It'll keep you dry, that's the main thing," said Denis, "once you get wet, it's a bugger to get dry again when you've got nowhere to go."

Just then another 'wanderer' joined them and said, "oh, hello Stringer, didn't notice you there. Who's this Charlie then?"

"Hello, Bob and that's his name, Charlie," said Denis, "where's Eddie, haven't seen around much lately?"

Bob, whose nick name was Dobby Bobby, for a reason that Denis have never discovered, usually hung out with a mate of his called Leddy Eddie and they were the brunt of many jokes, particularly with the 'winos' (homeless alcoholics) who used try and say the names as fast as they could. This usually started OK as Dobby Bobby and Leddy Eddie but ended up as being Bodee Ledee before they all collapsed because it was so funny when you'd had a drink.

Denis related this to Charlie who burst out laughing, "Dobby Bobby and Leddy Eddie, you couldn't make this up," he said.

Bob was saying "Eddie ain't been too good lately and they took him into hospital last week. The cold and what not were doing him no good at all."

"Oh, sorry to hear that," said Denis, "will he be in long?"

"Naw, should be out in a day or two. You know Eddie, he's pretty tough underneath. That's how he got his nick name you know? He used to say 'let 'im try that with me' and it used to get faster and faster when he was threatened and so it came out as led 'im, led 'e, which eventually became leddy."

"Underneath what?" said Charlie, "all the grime and dirt that you people seem to accumulate all over yourselves?"

Denis said, "ignore him, Bob, he's just an ignorant and bad-mannered wide boy who got caught thieving and is no better than you or I whatever he might think."

Bob just nodded looking at Charlie and said, "well I was right about his name wasn't I? Acts like a Charlie and is a proper Charlie."

Charlie was spluttering, "now listen you two, I don't need you, you...you...sanctimonious little shits......"

"I'd stop there if I were you," said Denis, "you need to get it through that thick head of yours that your arrogant 'great I am' ain't gonna cut any ice 'round here – you got that?"

Charlie just stood there with his mouth open as Denis went on, "you won't last five minutes unless you listen to the likes of me and Bob. We've been on the streets for a while now and know where the handouts are likely to be and where you can get a bit of kip."

"What like that Church Hall you took me to the other night, or perhaps the squat we've just vacated, very salubrious I don't think," said Charlie with a sneer.

"Oo,.. you got in the Church Hall the other night, you lucky sods. I had to content myself with the cardboard at the back of Sainsburys. It's not all bad though because sometimes they give you out-of-date stuff to eat, so it ain't that bad I suppose. Mind you there are a bunch of young kids who go around beating up the homeless just for the fun of it, the bastards. Some say it's the shop employing them to like, get rid of us, but I don't think it is."

Charlie looked from one to the other, dumbfounded. For once in his life he didn't have a witty comeback or some sort of disparaging comment to make.

"Oh, look it's stopped," said Bob, "I'm off to see Eddie later on. Might see you around perhaps?"

Denis said, "give Eddie my regards and I hope he's out and about soon."

Bob said, "will do," as he walked out of the railway arch.

Charlie was still shaking his head as though he was trying to clear his mind about something.

"What is it?" asked Dennis.

"I dunno if I'm ever gonna be able to do this," said Charlie.

"Yes you are," replied Denis, "you're already talking more like us than your poncey self yesterday. Come on, let's have a walk around the park. It's beginning to brighten up and I don't think we'll get any more kip tonight."

"It's still bleedin' freezin'," Charlie was saying as they stepped out of the railway arch and crossed back over the road to the small, inner city, park.

They walked around the park, for a little while, without saying a great deal to each other until they came to a bench, which didn't look too wet, and decided to sit down. Denis got some newspaper from a nearby bin and wiped off the remaining wet from the bench and they sat there with their hands in their pockets looking out on the rest of the park.

The park was really only a couple of football pitches and some open green spaces surrounded by a variety of different trees. Although the trees had lost all their leaves and were waiting for the next spring it was still a pleasant enough outlook and the sun had started to make a watery appearance although it was still quite cold.

As Denis looked at the newspapers that he had used to dry the bench he noticed some vouchers on a couple of the pages. He started to look through what pieces of the newspapers he had and the date at the top of each page. He soon had some vouchers for betting on horse racing that afternoon in the local branches of a national book-making chain or turf accountant as they like to call themselves these days.

As it was a Saturday there were lots of races and although the vouchers tended to be for specific races he thought it was definitely worth a punt as they say. He said to Charlie, "look at these Charlie."

"What are they? Food Stamps or something?" said Charlie not really that interested.

"No better than that," said Denis with a grin, "we can make a bit of money out of these."

"And how are you planning to do that then?" asked Charlie.

"Well there's a branch of a national chain of bookmakers on the High Street, just round the corner. So we'll go and have a look at the racing pages in there, we'll be able to have a warm in there as well. Then we pick out the horses to back and use these vouchers for the stake."

Charlie looked at the vouchers with renewed interest but then said, "these are just for 'wins'. The chances of picking out several winners with these vouchers is pretty thin."

"Ah but that's where you're wrong see? said Denis, "both you and me place the bets and so we can have 'two bites of the cherry' like and then we'll have got a much better chance of winning."

Charlie wasn't convinced but said, "anything to get a bit warmer even if we don't win. Come on, let's go."

As they were walking towards the High Street, Denis kept looking in shop windows to try and smarten himself up a bit. He hadn't had a shave for a few days although his clothes didn't look too dirty. Charlie seemed OK, he hadn't had chance to become as scruffy as some of the others yet thought Denis.

CHAPTER 13
Place your bets please

They arrived at the bookies a few minutes later and as Denis had promised it was warm inside. The book-making clerks looked them over as they entered the shop but Denis and Charlie ignored them and made their way over to the newspaper pages displayed on the walls and started to study 'the form'.

Charlie was saying that he knew very little about horse racing although he'd been on several corporate hospitality events to the Cheltenham Gold Cup.

"Well didn't you learn anything about the 'sport of Kings' there? Asked Denis.

"No, I was too busy getting pissed to notice what was going on it could have been greyhounds racing for all I knew about it."

"Now that's an idea," said Denis, "there's a voucher here for a greyhound race. It's for a 'forecast' which means we need to predict the first and second and in this case, in the right order."

"That'll take a bit of doing," said Charlie.

"Not necessarily, there's only 6 dogs to choose from. Let's go and have a look at the greyhound pages over there," Denis was saying as he wondered off further into the shop.

"Here we are," said Denis, "last race this morning. What do you fancy?"

Charlie just shrugged and said, "I'll leave it to you Denis, the way my luck is at the moment I don't think I could pick my nose let alone a winner."

Denis nodded and picked up a betting slip and completed the £1 forecast which the voucher was for. He took it to the bookies counter window and waited for his receipt and as there was only a few minutes to go before the race Denis and Charlie took up positions near one of the wall mounted, televisions that would be showing the race.

They looked at the screen as the dogs came out onto the race-track and one of the greyhounds they had backed did an almighty crap and Dennis said, "that's a good sign Charlie, he's a lot lighter now."

Charlie just nodded and they both looked on as the dogs were placed in their respective 'traps'.

"We're on trap numbers one and six," said Denis, as the dogs were released and started chasing after the electric rabbit.

They both starting chanting, "c'mon one and six, c'mon one and six."

The dogs flew round the track and in a couple of minutes it was apparent that one and six had come nowhere!

"Never mind," said Dennis jokingly, "we've got plenty more vouchers where that one came from."

"Looks like we're going to need them," replied Charlie.

Moving over to the horse racing pages they started to study the owners, the trainers and the jockeys and how the horses had got on in their last few races. It was difficult to spot a horse with good form and with decent odds. The better the horse the shorter the odds but as they weren't betting with real money, just the vouchers Denis thought they could perhaps be a bit more adventurous.

Charlie just stood there not looking too convinced that this was going to bring in any money. All he could think about was food, not really having any breakfast to speak of, in fact not eating anything since yesterday.

So, having decided on the selections, Denis placed the bets;

In the 12:30 a horse called 'Alright Now' at 7 to 1 seemed a good possibility and if it won he would get £8 back having placed the £1 win voucher.

In the 13:45 it was a horse called 'Another One' and at 15 to 1 was a bit of a long shot but if would return £16 using the other £1 win voucher for that particular race meeting.

Denis returned to Charlie who was looking at the TV screens as the 12:30 race was about to get under way.

Denis said, "these are the betting slips which will get us out of this hole we're currently wallowing in."

"I admire your faith," said Charlie, "so long as it's enough to get us something to eat, I'm absolutely starving."

The 12:30 started and the betting shop initially became quite as the TV commentator shouted "they're off!"

'Alright Now' lagged a little way behind the leaders but this was quite a long race Denis was saying to Charlie as shouts of 'c'mon get going' and so on were made at the TV screen.

Charlie and Denis were shouting along with the rest as 'Alright Now' entered that last furlong ahead of the field. They were jumping up and down and shouting and shouting and 'Alright Now' romped home, to use the expression.

"Great," said Charlie, "let's go and get something to eat."

"You won't get much with the £8 we've got coming and anyway now we're off and running so to speak, I think we need to keep on betting," said Dennis.

"But I'm starving," said Charlie.

"Just think of the slap-up meal we can have later if we get a few more bets to come up," replied Denis as he made his way over to the counter to collect his winnings.

As it was a Saturday there were a lot of races to look at and Denis decided the £8 would be best 'invested' over three races using accumulator bets whereby if one horse won then that would roll over to be bet on the next horse and so on. Denis assured Charlie that this was the only way to make some real money.

Denis studied the form from the newspaper pages on the walls of the bookies as Charlie just stood there muttering to himself about how he could 'eat a horse' never mind backing one.

Denis placed the bets and they waited in front of the TV screens to see the 13:45 race. The horse that they had backed was a bit of an outsider but had a good trainer and jockey. Again as the race started people were shouting for the horses they had backed. 'Another One' led from about halfway round the course and by the time it went through the winning post Charlie and Denis were almost 'horse' themselves, they had been cheering and shouting him on as he won at 15 to 1 odds.

"Bloody hell, Denis," said Charlie, "that's £16 we've got coming back." Making it sound like the millions of pounds that he used to deal with.

"I know," said Denis still unable to believe his luck.

"What shall we do with it," said Charlie.

What's all this 'we' stuff? I'm the one doing all the work here. You wouldn't be arsed to give me the time of day under normal circumstances. I bet you can't believe you're this excited about winning £16 - the amount of money that's gone through your hands over the years." Denis said.

"Look, Denis, I know I've been a bit of a prat since meeting you but it's only my reaction to the shock of being homeless and hungry."

"All right," said Denis, "it's fifty: fifty, providing you let me decide on the bets and what we're going to do with the money. We'll get something to eat this evening when the bookies close."

"But that's hours away," protested Charlie.

"I know but it will be worth it," Denis replied, "we're on a winning streak and you never, ever interrupt a winning streak!"

So the £16 was used for further bets and as the accumulator bets started to 'come in' Denis and Charlie realised that not only would they have enough for a meal but also they would be able to pay for a somewhere to sleep that night.

The bookies finally closed at 6:00pm although the last race had finished a short time before. The bookies had to take time cashing up because Denis and Charlie had won so much money that it threatened to leave the bookies without their usual cash float once they had paid out. The book makers couldn't believe that they had had such luck. They had never seen anything like it and the one said to Denis, "I thought we might have to give you a cheque but it looks like we can just about cover your winnings."

Charlie estimated that they had several thousands of pounds stuffed into their pockets by the time they left the bookies, both with huge grins on their faces.

CHAPTER 14
Saturday Night

Charlie and Dennis were halfway down the road when they realised that it was dark and that they needed somewhere to stay and as Charlie kept reminding Denis they hadn't eaten all day.

Denis said, "there's a nice little B&B down here where we can stay at tonight. They've usually got rooms available."

"A B&B," said Charlie, "are you kidding? With all this cash we can book into a fancy hotel and have room service and such like and….."

"Blow the lot," added Denis, "look Charlie, if we're ever gonna get out of this mess we're in then we've got to look after the money so that we'll have enough to get back into the real world and not the cardboard cities that I've had to live with in the past!"

"But…."

"No buts Charlie," Denis was saying, "I know we said fifty: fifty of the winnings but as I did the most of the work in getting the money, I think it's only fair that I should have the main say in how we spend it from now on, at least for the time being. Don't you?"

"Oh, alright Denis," said Charlie reluctantly, "we'll book into the B&B then. But can we then please, please get something to eat!"

They soon arrived at Mrs Johnson's B&B just off the High Street. Although there were only a few rooms to let, there were two vacant which Denis and Charlie secured for £30 each. Neither had got any luggage and initially had trouble convincing Mrs Johnson that they could actually afford to pay for the rooms. Once money had changed hands she was more accommodating and pointed out the bathroom and informed them of the charges for baths and hot water which she suggested they might want to use as soon as they had paid her. They weren't sure if they would be stopping for two nights – Saturday and Sunday, and said they would see what happened tomorrow before paying out for a further night now. So they paid Mrs Johnson for the one night plus hot water charges.

Denis and Charlie were thinking that they would be able to make some more money on Monday or perhaps tomorrow depending on what races were on. They both had big plans for how they were going to spend it, although these plans didn't always coincide with one another.

But, for now, it was Saturday night and they'd had a bit of a wash and brush up and so it was time to get something to eat. Of course they couldn't agree where to go or what to have. Denis was thinking fish and chips, or pie and chips or anything with chips really provided it 'filled the gap' whereas Charlie thought some five-star gourmet restaurant was more his style.

Denis was saying, "it's just a con you know? The gourmet means that you'll still be hungry afterwards. You need a real 'gut filler' because you may not be able to afford it much longer depending on how we get on tomorrow and Monday."

"Oh, I've got big plans for this money I have," said Charlie, "and, anyway, what's wrong with wanting a bit of a treat tonight after the day we've had today?"

"Well, I want a decent, filling meal. Not some poncy noveau cuisine where it looks like a work of art but two mouthfuls later it's gone! I guessed you'd probably come up with something like that but it's not gonna happen. It's going to be somewhere 'cheap and cheerful' tonight, where you can get a proper diner, OK?" replied Denis.

"A 'proper dinner', what are you on about?" said Charlie.

"I like a decent, good value meal, I'm funny like that," said Denis sarcastically.

Eventually they settled on a 'greasy spoon' café tucked away down a side street. It obviously, mainly catered for the working week workers but tried to offer a Saturday night special. What it termed as a 'dining experience' which it never quite pulled off. There were net curtains halfway up the windows to give the diners a little privacy. The tables were off a particularly resilient formica which looked like it had been there since the 1950s (which it probably had). It was usually a self-service establishment where the customer went up to the counter to order and pay for their food and then a few minutes later whoever was serving would bellow out their order ready for collection.

However on a Saturday night the café provided waiter service of sorts and, as it was licensed, alcoholic drinks were served although they didn't stretch to a wine waiter mainly because they served beer rather than wine. The owners had started it all off as a bit of pretentious place to go on a Saturday hoping to attract a better class of customer. However what they got was the likes of Denis and Charlie and others who looked like life wasn't treating them too kind at the moment. The main thing was it was decent and filling food accompanied by a beer or two.

There were photos on the walls of East End boxers who had made it good during the 1950s which showed them in the ring and receiving championship awards, cups and belts and so on. There were also stills from gangster films which had been filmed at the café as it truly represented a step back in time.

Denis and Charlie found a small table towards the back of the place. It was only small and had about two dozen tables and surprisingly, for a Saturday night, was almost full.

Denis said, "times must be worse than what we thought judging by the number of people in here on a Saturday night. It only ever used to be open during the week because most punters took themselves up West at the weekends. It just shows how times have changed."

"It's not surprising with all the do-gooders and the amount of red tape you have to navigate through. That's what brought me down, you know, and it looks like others haven't done much better, looking at this crowd." replied Charlie.

"Now Charlie, let's not get carried away, we both know you were a crook and you got caught. If you'd been a bit more compassionate about how you did business you might have got away with it. But, let's face it, you were a nasty, ruthless bastard, that most people were glad to see the back of."

"Don't sugar coat it, Denis, give it to me straight, why don't you?" said Charlie somewhat affronted, "I'm sure I wasn't as bad as you make out. It was just a bit of bad luck and a bit of a misunderstanding and......."

"Don't give me that," Denis interrupted, "you were a right bastard and you know it! I suspect you even enjoyed it didn't you? All that unbridled power that you thought you had."

Charlie stared at Denis and said, "do you really think I was a bad as all that?"

"Aye, that and worse probably," said Denis, "you need to look at your current situation as a chance for you to redeem yourself. Try and be a bit nicer to people, not because they can help you but because you want to help them for a change."

"Well, I can try, I suppose. After all it is getting near to Christmas" Charlie was saying as their food arrived.

"Pie and chips twice and two bottles of brown ale?" said the waiter.

"Yeah that's us," said Charlie with a grimace, "thanks."

"There you are that wasn't so difficult to do, was it?" said Denis, "being polite and saying please and thank you can get you a long way you know."

They followed the pie and chips with homemade, gut filling, bread and butter pudding and custard. The café had no sense of portion control and the puddings arrived in two enormous dishes.

"There's enough to feed a family of four here," said Charlie getting 'stuck' into his dessert.

"Get it down your neck," replied Denis, "you never know when you are going to be hungry again and you would be glad of it then and no mistake I can tell you."

So they finished their puddings with another bottle of beer and when the bill arrived they couldn't believe it was so cheap and so left a couple of pounds as a tip for the waiter who, whilst not exactly surly, wasn't too friendly either.

It was still relatively early and Charlie suggested that they pop into the pub on the corner near their digs to have a couple of pints as a nightcap.

Denis nodded and said, "lead on."

CHAPTER 15
In the pub

"What shall we do tomorrow?" asked Charlie.

"Well, I think we'll have to have a reckon up and see if any of the bookies are open. There is some racing now on a Sunday and so we might be able to have a few more bets," replied Denis.

"Don't you think that's pushing our luck a bit?" said Charlie, "I mean shouldn't we leave it for a day or so before we get back to gambling away what we have?"

Denis thought for a moment and said, "I think we need to see if our luck will hold out. We hit on a winning streak today and there's no reason why it shouldn't continue tomorrow, but you never know. Luck can be a funny thing you know. You interrupt a winning streak and it just goes away. Still we'll know tomorrow if we can do any good.

"OK, Denis I'll leave it to you, but if we do win big then I want a say in how we invest it," said Charlie.

"Oh, yeah, another of your get rich quick schemes is it?" Denis replied.

"No, I'm not going down that route again. I think I might have finally learned my lesson. I'm going to try and do things on the 'up and up' from now on and if I step out of line I want you to tell me. I've a feeling our luck is changing and I don't want to cock it up this time." said Charlie.

"It's funny thing isn't it, 'Luck' that is?" said Denis, I've met some really lucky people and conversely some really unlucky buggers, who no matter what they do, it just never seems to turn out right for them."

Charlie thought for a moment before saying, "Yeah, it's like one of those things where you either have it or you don't. You can't see it, feel it or touch it – it's just there. If you've got it you don't particularly need anything else and as some people say 'it's better to be lucky than good'. D'you know when I was a rising star at FinCo people used to say to me 'you're lucky, you are' or something like, 'you've got a charmed life', but I used to work my socks off. I know you don't think I've done a day's work in my life but I could work up to twenty hours a day and sometimes I was working seven days a week!"

Denis said, "yes it's a strange thing alright. I think it was a golfer who said something like, 'the harder you work at it the luckier you get', and I suppose that's true in a way. But I've known people, not many, it's true, but some people are born lucky. We used to have a saying about one bloke I knew that if he fell off the roof of a tall building he would fall into a new suit, that's how lucky he was. He still is for all I know, I haven't seen him for years. But he and I used to be in for the same jobs and guess who always used to get them? He could win on the horses, the lottery, all sorts. Not vast amounts of money but enough to keep him 'comfortable' as he used to say."

"Tell me Denis," asked Charlie, "what was it that you used to do?"

Denis looked at Charlie and said, "well I was basically in the same game as you. You know financial services and such like. Not as high flying as you, but providing advice on finance and investments, that sort of thing. I had a partner and he was a crook, a bit like you. He...."

"Now that's uncalled for, I said I've made a lot of mistakes but I was no petty crook!" butted in Charlie.

"Oh, I know that Charlie, you stole the big bucks," Denis continued, "and my business partner was similar to you although not in the same league. It wasn't what he'd done or the money for that matter, which to me, by the way, was a fairly substantial sum, but it was the deceit that really shocked me. I thought we shared the same ideals of honesty and fair dealing..."

"As they say once you can fake that you've got it made," interrupted Charlie.

"No not exactly, I did genuinely believe that we could provide valuable services in a straightforward and honest way and still make money. I still believe that today. You don't have to cheat people to make a few quid." Denis said with feeling.

"So what happened?" asked Charlie.

"My partner, psychedelic Stanley, as he became known. He didn't like to be called that but he ended up snorting so much stuff up his nose that he usually wasn't very coherent. Although that didn't stop him fiddling the accounts. He was siphoning off larger and larger amounts of money mainly to pay for his coke habit but also to put aside in his own personal bank accounts. The reports I got through showed that the money was still there, in the business bank accounts, and, as I was the main director of the company, it was assumed that I was in on the scams he pulled. Stan had squirrelled away so much money into his own personal accounts that the first I knew of it was when a cheque was returned 'refer to drawer' meaning there was no money left in an account which should have hundreds of thousands of pounds according to my records."

"Wow, that must have some as a bit of a shock," Charlie said.

"It wasn't so much the shock but the sequence of events which followed and which followed rather quickly I might add. Within a couple of weeks, word had got round and everyone wanted their money back and the company had to go into liquidation. I was declared bankrupt because of personal liability lawsuits which claimed negligence on my part. So there were also criminal charges likely to be brought against me. Like you, my wife left me, and I lost my house, car and everything else. I later found out that my wife had shacked up with Stan and that she must have known what was coming because she had been putting things in her name, you know, our share portfolio, bank accounts and such like. So bankruptcy hit hard and swift. I was destitute and homeless and a bit older that what you are now, which made it even harder to get back on my feet. The only good thing was that my kids were off at university and so never saw the humiliation."

Charlie looked at Denis and said, "sorry to hear that mate, when was all this then?"

"Oh getting on for about four or five years ago or so now. You tend to lose track of time when you don't have a proper working life, or any type of life to come to that. I've had one or two temporary jobs and I've managed to get off the streets a couple of times as well. But there's one thing I've learned and that is that it's really expensive being poor!" Denis went on, "I've sort of fallen into a rut these past few months and I'm finding it difficult to get out of it and try and look on the bright side…."

"All ways look on the bright side of life, di di di…", sang Charlie.

Denis looked at him and said, "very droll, I don't think, that don't help Charlie. I tell you what though, when you arrived the other day, it brought it all back to me. Believe it or not I was just like you when I first hit the streets. In shock, finding it hard to actually believe that something like that could happened to me. I kept thinking over and over again, how could this happen to me. It just wasn't right somehow and I looked at other people to blame. Of course there was no one else to blame but myself for being so naïve. The authorities couldn't believe anyone could be so stupid and so they thought that I must have condoned Stan's thieving and, he had covered his tracks well and so it did end up looking as though it was me who had had their hands in the till and not him! Fortunately, I'd got a good brief from the public defender's office who was very sympathetic and he manged to get me off the criminal charges but I was banned from running a company or being a director for a number of years. I was a social outcast because you know how people think – 'there's no smoke without fire'- so everyone thought I was as guilty as hell. Meanwhile, Stan and Lucy, that was my wife's name, had it away abroad somewhere and were no doubt smashed out of their brains on coke whilst I was walking the streets."

"What did you do?" asked Charlie.

"Well you pretty soon learn to adapt, you have to otherwise you wouldn't last five minutes. All I'd got were the clothes on me back and a couple of pounds which I'd managed to hide. But it didn't last very long and so I was sleeping rough just like what we were doing last week. It's not so bad in the summer when the weather's good but you saw yourself what it was like last week – enough to freeze the nuts of a brass monkey." Denis carried on, a faraway look in his eye. "I don't mind telling you that I sailed pretty close to the mark with a bit of shoplifting and thieving. It was the only way I could survive and in a way I just didn't care if I got caught."

Charlie said, "Where did you go Denis?"

"Oh round and about, not too far. You like to stay close to the district you know and I did manage to get one or two temporary jobs and so I could pay for a B&B, like Mrs Johnson's, when I was working. Only menial stuff but it brought in a few quid and there was always the chance of working a scam or two." Denis said.

"Scams? You?" said Charlie, "and you're always telling me about being honest and upright."

Denis replied, "its nothing I'm proud of but when you're first made homeless you can still look the part and still have the confidence to pull it off but after a while that fades and you can no longer cut it as a con man."

"So what sort of scams did you pull then Denis?" asked Charlie.

"Mostly short scams. You know the sort you go into a jewellers and ask to try on rings or look at necklaces for the wife and then when they have a lot of stuff out on the counter you try and confuse them so that you can pocket a few pieces without them noticing. It was OK at first but they started to get wise to it and so I couldn't do that one anymore," Denis explained.

Charlie said, "people just aren't as trusting as they used to be."

"I don't blame them, there's so much naughty stuff going on these days. It's just got out of hand. D'you know that at one time I could buy a packet of fags and insist that I'd given the shop-keeper a £20 note and so got the change from a score rather than the tenner that I'd actually given him." sighed Denis.

Denis was clearly distressed and so Charlie thought it better to move on to more positive subjects like what would they would do if ever they were in the position of having a bit of 'real money' again. They talked about this, rather wistfully, till it was the pub's closing time and they staggered back to the B&B.

CHAPTER 16
Sunday

Denis woke early on the Sunday morning and had a quick wash and got dressed before banging on Charlie's door.

"C'mon Charlie," Denis shouted, "we've got to get going or we'll be charged for another day before we've started."

Charlie opened the door looking a bit worse for wear which had something to do with him sleeping in his clothes and also something to do with the six pints of Guinness he downed in the pub the night before.

"What time is it?" he said.

"It's still early but we need to be out and about before the breakfast queues start," replied Denis.

Charlie looked horrified and said, "we're not going back to that Shelter place are we?"

"No," said Denis, "I think we can stretch to something a bit more appetising than that."

"I need to get some toiletries and stuff," said Charlie as he got ready to go out, "I mean I've got nothing but these clothes that I'm wearing and I think they're beginning to pong a bit."

"Well the shops don't open until ten o'clock on Sundays and so we'll go and have breakfast first and then get what we need," replied Denis.

So saying a 'goodbye' to Mrs Johnson, who looked a bit relieved at first to see them go and then horrified when they said that they might be back later.

Charlie and Denis strode purposefully along the High Street looking for breakfast. The first place they came across was a

McDonalds and as Charlie was complaining about his stomach thinking his throat was cut they decided to go and have a couple of big breakfasts in there.

After two, big breakfasts each and unlimited coffee they ventured forth in search of the shops.

Denis bought a complete new outfit, shirt, trousers, coat and most importantly shoes. He threw his old stuff away because it was not only dirty, but threadbare as well, and his old shoes had more holes in the soles than sole in the holes so to speak.

Charlie needed some toiletries and underwear and both of them filled a couple of ruck sacks with what they needed. Even after paying for the stuff they were still left with a fairly big stake for betting on the horses.

They went back along the High Street to the bookies that they had had such success with yesterday, just in time for its opening. Only to be told by the bookies that they couldn't serve them anymore. After the amount they'd won yesterday they were banned. They explained that it was the head office which had looked at the returns yesterday and when they told them what had happened they said no more bets from Denis and Charlie

"Good init?" said Denis, "They're quick enough to take your money but when it comes to paying out they won't let you even have a bet in case they've got to pay out! Some sportsmen they are!"

Charlie and Denis came out of the book-makers and looked for another one. There was a another one down the road and so they went in there. There weren't that many races on this particular Sunday afternoon in December and Denis wasn't sure if all of the bookies would be open and so were glad that this one was willing to let them place their bets.

"How much have we got?" asked Charlie.

"Enough for some good bets," replied Denis, "let's have a look at what's racing," as he moved towards the walls with that day's newspaper racing pages pinned up. Charlie looked on as Denis studied the form moving from one meeting to another displayed on the different newspaper pages pinned to the walls.

"I think what we'll do," said Denis, "is back a number of horses in an accumulator bet....."

"like we did yesterday," Charlie jumped in.

"Yeah, but this time we will do a number of different Yankee bets, together with other accumulators, as well as single win bets," said Denis.

"I haven't a clue about what you just said," replied Charlie, "but so long as it brings in the dough, then go for it."

Charlie played the fruit machines whilst Denis placed the bets. His luck was definitely changing as he was up quite a bit when there was an almighty row over by the counter. Denis was remonstrating with the clerk and the clerk was shaking his head. Charlie went over to see what the problem was.

"What's the matter Denis," said Charlie.

"This prat won't pay us out," Denis almost shouted. "I placed the bets in good faith and now his saying that I can't have won so much money with such small stakes!"

The clerk said, "you've had all you're going to get from us. The shop up the road warned us about a couple of con men who were winning large sums of money yesterday....."

"We won that money fair and square," interrupted Denis.

"Well there's no more for you here so sling your hook," the clerk replied.

"C'mon Denis, let's go," said Charlie, "you can't argue with this likes of them and remember the only bet enforceable in law is one placed on the racecourse, at the actual day of the race itself, even if we could take them to court."

"Bastards!" shouted Denis, "I should be picking up thousands now instead of what you've given me."

"Think yourself lucky you've got that before we spotted who you were. No one likes a cheat you know?" said the clerk.

"And no ones likes a bookie who welches on his bet," retorted Charlie, "it's just not the gentlemanly thing to do you know."

So they walked out of the bookies. Denis in a huff and Charlie walking like John Wayne because his pockets were full of the £1 pound coins he'd won on the fruit machines.

Once outside, Denis jumped in the air and said, "we've got most of the money Charlie, there's only a couple of races to go and even if we'd got winners in both of them it wouldn't have made a great deal of difference to the final amount that's in my pockets."

"Well, how much have you got?" said Charlie who was pleased with the few hundred in his pockets.

Denis said, "we've got the best part of £50,000 from yesterday and today!"

"Get away," said Charlie, "It can't be that much, can it?"

"I was putting £100 each way, accumulator bets on long odds which means that provided a horse was placed we basically got our money back but when that one race came in, and together with the three winners we already had, then we had a total pay-out of 14 bets. They'd paid this out before they realised and I think it was because the shop was running short of money again, like yesterday, when they decided to pull the plug. But I had that accumulator and a couple of wins as well and so with what was left from yesterday's money it must be nigh on fifty grand!" Denis grinned.

"Let's see if we can book into a hotel tonight as we look a bit more respectful than yesterday," said Charlie.

"OK," said Denis, "there's a decent hotel over there." Indicating a rather large building that was part of a national chain of Holiday Inns.

CHAPTER 17
The Holiday Inn

The receptionists gave Charlie and Denis a bit of a suspicious look when they asked for a couple of rooms. At £150 night it wasn't the cheapest accommodation but it did include a full breakfast and so they thought that they'd go for it.

There was a bit of a discussion about them not having credit cards but as Charlie and Denis were willing to, not only pay cash, but to also to leave a deposit against any extras, the receptionists then decided that would be OK and let them have the rooms.

Charlie and Denis went up to their rooms. They had no luggage save for a couple of rucksacks and quickly settled in. Denis went to Charlie's room for the big' reckon up' as he called it and sure enough, after a couple of recounts there was just a few pounds short of £50,000.

"Let's go and have some dinner Denis, and discuss what to do with the money."

Denis replied, "OK, and we need to think this through, it's a good enough stake to get us both back on our feet again."

In the dining room the two of them started talking about outlandish schemes before reality got a grip and they settled down to more realistic propositions. They had their dinner and continued talking well into the night about how to use the money to make a 'comeback' as Charlie kept saying.

Denis said, "I don't want either of us to make the same mistakes as we did last time. This time it's all gotta be 'above board', completely honest and transparent and with the necessary checks and balances to cover both of us."

"Are you saying you don't trust me?" asked Charlie.

"It's not a question of trust. We have to do things the right way to protect us both," said Denis. "Anyway, I think you've learned from your mistakes and, although it pains me to say it, I think you've become a much nicer person since you haven't had any money. So I think you'll behave yourself this time."

Charlie thought for a moment and said, "you're right you know Denis, I have learned my lesson and I will behave better from now on, you have my word on that. Once I'm back on top again, I won't make the same mistakes this time."

"I believe you, for once, Charlie," said Denis, "it's now just how we go about it. We're going to need an address and so I think we'll have to rent somewhere to live first of all. We can then use this address to form a company. I think my ban from being a director has expired, how about you, are there any legal restrictions that we need to take into account?"

"No, I was never banned for any great time, as such, from being a company director because it was a personal bankruptcy," Charlie said.

"OK then, first thing tomorrow, let's go round to an estate agents to get us a property that we can rent and move into straightway. It'll need to be furnished because we can't be faffing about buying furniture and stuff when we'll be trying to get a business off the ground," Denis continued. "I think we'll have to give all our old contacts a swerve, my contacts won't remember me and yours won't want to remember you!"

"That's below the belt that is Denis," protested Charlie, "a lot of my contacts made a lot of money because of me!"

Denis looked at Charlie and said, "Charlie, you've got to realise that your old life has gone. People are not going to want to know you now because of the stigma attached to being a bankrupt and also because you got caught out. You pulled too many strokes in the past and people will still think you're trying to get away with as much as possible. It doesn't matter how much of a reformed character you are now, the sort of business we're going in needs the utmost trust and not to put too fine a point on things your old contacts don't trust you anymore."

Charlie just nodded. He knew Denis was right but it still rankled with him when he remembered how he used to be what was known in those days as a 'mover and shaker'. The Americans used to coin an expression 'Masters of the Universe' and that is exactly how Charlie used to see himself in those days. But now, he thought, what am I now?

After a bit too much to drink again Charlie and Denis said good-night and retired to their rooms where both of them had the best night's sleep for quite a while.

CHAPTER 18
A new day dawns

Both Charlie and Denis were up well in time for the breakfast which was a buffet laid out in the dining room of the Holiday Inn. Like most large modern hotels it was completely impersonal and other than bringing toast and coffee the waitresses left them to it. They both stuffed themselves silly with bacon and eggs and sausages and all the other items of the full English breakfast. Denis had got into the habit of eating just as much as he could as he never knew when his next meal would be. Charlie was still suffering hunger pangs from the week before where he had to adjust his diet to be whatever he could get his hands on and which invariably was never enough.

After breakfast they checked out and retrieved the balance of cash not used from their deposit. They were both in a buoyant mood as they strolled back along the High Street to look in the local estate agents windows. The second one they came to seemed to specialise more in the rental market and they had a couple of properties that they arranged for Charlie and Denis to view straight away.

The first one was a flat and was very nicely decorated and furnished but the address left no doubt that it was a residential property and so reluctantly they couldn't proceed with that. They then looked at the second property which was a house. The address was number 12 on the main road and this would suit their needs for a business address although the house itself needed a bit of a 'freshen up' as Denis kept saying. But the furniture was adequate and it was clean enough and so they said they would sign the rental agreement straightaway.

They moved in on that Monday afternoon and sorted who would have what bedroom, after a fair bit of squabbling. They did some shopping for food and supplies, both needed laptop computers and stationery as well. So they bought what was necessary and they would then have a few clear days to get started on their business.

The house already had a broadband hub and they called the telecoms company to get connected which was like trying to wrestle with water. It took a psychologically damaging amount of time and because they were frequently being cut off a red mist descended and Charlie became almost homicidal.

Now that they had an address they could open a bank account which could have proved trickier than what it was. They way banks are these days they get so twitchy about things and Charlie was saying, "it isn't even their money and they're giving us a hard time," when Denis said, "leave it to me Charlie."

"Hello Judge, how are you doing?" said Denis, "haven't seen you for a long time?"

"It's Malcolm Teigh now," said the Judge.

He'd been called the Judge at the Shelter when Denis had first met him because he was a disbarred solicitor who had had it away with clients money. He'd manage to escape going to prison but had a two-year suspended sentence hanging over him. Malcolm was very tall, well over six foot and so tended to stand out from a crowd- not something that was desirable when he was 'working the cons'. But it did give him a certain amount of gravitas as a bank employee. He wore a suit, had a good haircut and looked the part of the gentleman banker.

Denis thought for a minute and said, "that's bit obvious isn't it? M.Teigh, as in empty?"

Malcolm said, "listen that's what they know me as here so don't get cocking it up for me. What do you want anyway?"

"How did you manage to end up working here? I thought you still had an outstanding suspended sentence hanging over you?"

"Why don't you speak up and let them all know?" whispered Malcolm looking around to make sure that no one could overhear them. "I managed to get that bloke, Pebbles, you know him, he used to go to the Shelter now and again to create a few documents for me."

"Why was he called Pebbles?" asked Charlie.

"Because," said Denis, "he used to wear really think glasses, so thick in fact that they were like pebbles in front of his eyes. He was a bit of a weird bloke but one of the best forgers that I had ever seen."

"Carry on, don't mind me," said Malcolm, "did you just come in here to have a chat amongst yourselves and get me the sack?"

Charlie said, "he's bit touchy isn't he?"

"He's got to be careful with such a forged background and that," said Denis.

Malcolm sighed and said, "why don't you tell the whole bleedin' world? Was there something you wanted or have you just popped in to wind me up?"

Denis looked at Charlie and said, "we've come to the right bank Charlie. Malcolm will get us sorted, won't you Malcolm?"

"If you ever get round to telling me what you want I'll try and see what I can do for you," said Malcolm.

"We need two personal current accounts with linked saving and overnight deposit facility and the same for a business account. The name of the business is ChasDen Ltd. and we will need business credit cards and a share dealing account linked to it," Denis said.

Charlie added, "we'll be depositing about £40,000 now and we expect you to match this with a loan facility up to the same amount if needed."

Malcolm was making notes and said, "you don't want much do

you? I take it the usual background checks need to be circumvented in some way and that you'll need the cheque books and credit cards pretty swiftly?"

Denis said, "that's very perceptive of you Jud... Malcolm. We'll have the company formed at Companies House just as soon as we can get our own credit cards to pay for it."

"I might need to grease a few palms," said Malcolm, "so all of this might not come cheap and I need your assurance that you're not working the loans scam. I mean with your track record....."

"How much?" said Charlie and Denis together.

"Well, I'll need a couple of grand and there's a couple of blokes that'll need 'sweeteners' for, say a grand a piece although I might be able to get them for a monkey each," replied Malcolm.

Denis said, "that's a bit strong isn't it Malcolm, after all we know you. I mean £2,000 just to ease the path so to speak and another £2,000 for your mates. Let's say a monkey for you and leave it at a pony a piece for both of them and any more than the £50 can come out of your monkey, OK?"

"You drive a hard bargain Strin... Denis," said Malcolm, "but I couldn't do it for less than a grand for me and a ton for each of me 'associates'."

"OK agreed, there'll be £1,200 in an envelope for you when we come in to pick up the cheque books and credit cards," said Denis.

Malcolm shook his head and said, "that won't work Denis, I need to grease the wheels beforehand if you see what I mean."

Charlie jumped in and said, "why don't you meet us in the pub on the corner, the one called the Red Lion, at about six tonight and we can settle up with you then?"

"OK," said Malcolm, "I'm just going to need signatures on a few of these forms and then I'll see you in the Red Lion this evening."

Denis and Charlie shook hands and said goodbye to Malcolm. As they left the bank Denis said, "well that's a turn up for the books. The Judge working in a bank."

"A bit of luck for us though Denis," said Charlie, "at least he should be able to skim over a few of the hurdles we would have had to jump through if we didn't know anyone. Do you think he's working a scam there?"

Denis thought for a moment and said, "no, not the Judge, he always swore blind he was innocent. Mind you everyone does don't they? But I think deep down he's honest or trying to be. Like a lot of people really."

Charlie said, "they reckon that the majority of people are honest only to the degree to which they could get away with anything. In other words most people are honest until given the opportunity to be dishonest. Couple that with greed and it's no wonder there are so many scams about."

"That's a bit philosophical for you isn't it Charlie?" replied Denis.

Charlie had a sort of smug look on his face and said, "perhaps I'm beginning to see the bigger picture. Now about this business of ours. Let me see if I've got it right."

"Let's get to the Red Lion and we can go through it all before the Judg... Malcolm arrives. We could probably run it past him as well and get his thoughts on it, after all he is a trained lawyer." said Denis.

CHAPTER 19
The Red Lion

Charlie and Denis realised that they hadn't had any lunch and so they ordered pie and chips with their pints of beer. They were still in the same frame of mind of eating what you can when you can because you don't know where your next meal comes from. If their plans worked out they wouldn't have to think this way for much longer.

They found a private booth, towards the back of the pub, and started to discuss the business and how they would proceed once Malcolm came through with the necessary banking requirements.

"You know," said Charlie, "with someone like Malcolm on the inside we could really clean up."

Denis looked at Charlie and said, "I thought we'd agreed that we were going legit this time around. You and I both know that there are any number of scams we could work with a 'tame' banker on our side. But we did agree Charlie that we'd play it straight and so, as much as the temptation is, I think we need to stick to the original plan."

Charlie replied, "it's just going to take a lot longer without perhaps cutting a few corners here and there. I mean everyone does it if they want to make some real money."

"No, Charlie, that's not the way. We've both been given a second chance and I don't want to blow it this time. We stick with being honest and trustworthy and don't abuse the chance we've been given," said Denis.

"OK, OK," said Charlie, "I was just saying that's all. You're right of course, and we will stick with the moral code as well as to the letter of the law. Now, we're going to need a post office box number as well as the house address. We'll need office space as soon as things start to take off as well."

Denis said, "now don't get ahead of yourself. Are you sure you still have the knack for this Charlie? I mean investing in derivatives and such like is a very specialised area and if you don't know what you are doing you can lose the lot."

"I know what I'm doing Denis," Charlie said rather confidently. "Derivatives are just bits of paper linked to underlying assets that's all. Price movements in the underlying asset are amplified in the derivative which in some cases can actually give you access to the asset, such as stocks and shares. I made enough money out of this type of investing before and I picked up some of the best ideas from the experts at FinCo. Once we have our necessary accounts set up, we start trading Certificates for Difference or CDs, as they are known, we also buy and sell both 'Call' and 'Put' options and finally we underpin it all with a bit of what's called spread betting and foreign exchange arbitrage. You must have come across some of these things in your time Denis?"

"Yeah, I do remember some of them," Denis replied, "when the 'greed is good' mantra and the 'Loadsamoney' philosophy was rife. In those days you couldn't go wrong because everything was going up as the markets expanded. I remember there was a saying at the time of all those utility privatisations that, 'if the government floated dog shit, it would still sell' and a lot of people did make a lot of money. But Charlie, the world has moved on and with automated trading systems and the like markets can move very quickly indeed and I don't want to be caught with my trousers down when the brown stuff hits the fan."

Charlie laughed and said, "with your luck at the moment Denis I don't think we'll go too far in the wrong direction. The CD's and the spread betting are a bit like the bets you were placing at the bookies. Instead of a horse, winning or losing, you are essentially betting on the price of say a share going up or down. There's no tax with this as any proceeds are classed as 'winnings'. The options are again generally linked to shares although you can get options in anything, commodities or other financial products. Basically the option is the right but not the obligation to either buy, a call option, or sell, a put option, the underlying share. As the options are traded then just a small movement in the underlying share price can change the price of the option significantly and so it can be sold on for a really big profit if you've got it right. Remember this is just the start once we establish a track record, and are making some 'real' money, then we kick off the investment funds and start to leverage up our gains."

"I wish you hadn't used that expression Charlie," Denis replied a bit subdued, "whenever there's 'leverage' involved there's usually more debt than sense and you can expect a load of trouble!"

"Have a little faith Denis," Charlie continued, "if we don't make enough to go that way we'll just stick to our own account and make returns offa that. An individual now can make the same sort of percentages that a big corporation can make, albeit not the same absolute amounts. All it needs is an internet connection, a few subscriptions and the willingness to take a bit of a risk."

Just then Malcolm arrived with the necessary account numbers, he confirmed that credit cards and cheque books were being produced and should be with them in a day or two. He said that it had cost him a bit more than a ton apiece to get things moving as Denis handed over the envelope with the £1200 in it.

"There's £1200 as agreed there Malcolm, so you'll have to square that out of your bung," said Denis, "it won't be the last time you'll be doing us favours and so there'll be more where that came from later. So what'll you have to drink?"

Malcolm just shook his head and said, "OK for now, but I expect you to make this up to me at some point and I'll have a very large whisky!"

Charlie went to get the drinks in whilst Denis and Malcolm reminisced about the 'old times' which actually wasn't that long ago but just seemed like it. They'd both been on the streets for quite a while and Denis was intrigued about the job Pebbles had done in forging the documentation for the Judge, Malcolm, to get a job in a bank of all places.

As Charlie returned with the drinks Denis was saying, "so it's all on the up-and-up now then Malcolm? No more working 'fast-ones'?"

Malcolm looked a bit aggrieved and said, "I'm glad I'm back in the mainstream side of things and I won't be jeopardising this little set up any time soon I can tell you."

Charlie butted in, "but if the price was right would you be willing to do a bit of naughty again?"

"You ain't working a scam are you?" said Malcolm looking over his shoulder, "I told you I'm going straight!"

"Alright, alright," said Denis, "Charlie was only asking, no harm done. We've just been exploring various business opportunities and Charlie remarked that with someone on the inside it would be real easy to work a few scams that's all."

Malcolm looked worried and said, "what d'you mean 'that's all'. I've put my neck on the line for you as it is and on the basis of you going legit."

Charlie said, "sorry Malcolm, I was just thinking aloud that's all."

"Well turn the bloody volume down then because I don't wanna know," protested Malcolm.

So the three of them had a few more drinks and chatted about this and that until it was time to get home. With the account numbers in their pockets it was to be a busy day for Denis and Charlie tomorrow.

CHAPTER 20
Let the 'games' begin

Charlie and Denis were both up early the next morning and went straight onto the various websites to register the new accounts needed to start trading. All of the registrations required deposits before they could trade and the £40,000 at the bank soon took a bit of a 'pounding'. They'd left enough walking around cash for food and drink and so felt that they could risk all of their bank stake in the 'game' as Charlie kept calling it. He kept saying that it was a lot different to when he started and the 'hoops you had to jump through' to get set up. Now as soon as you were registered then you were ready for the 'off'.

The ChasDen company had been registered at Companies House and a cheap and cheerful web site had been created for the business. Charlie decided to trade within the company and also as an individual reasoning that this would give a degree of flexibility and also enable them to hedge their bets.

First off was the spread betting which basically involved betting on shares and other tradable assets and such like going up or down. Each point in either direction was worth as much as a person was prepared to risk and there were 'stops' that could be applied so that if a share went into free fall you could bail out before it ruined you. Conversely the sky was literally the limit and even a small increase in prices could bring in big returns.

Denis was carrying out the necessary research using a couple of subscription web sites and Charlie was carrying out the trades. It was possible to trade several times on the same item in one day and so both of them were kept busy continually modifying their 'positions' as they were called.

They looked at the CDs but thought better of it and concentrated on the spread betting for the first day. They had all the accounts open ready to trade and Denis's research needed to be done at a pace so that they could 'get up to speed' with what was happening in the financial markets.

At the end of the first day they were ahead by a few thousand pounds much to the amazement of Denis. Charlie just grinned and said that he'd seen nothing yet and to wait until they started trading in a number of different markets and then the real money would start pouring in.

The next few days trading passed in a blur but produced similar results and the investments now included CDs, options and foreign exchange or Forex as Charlie like to call it. This was where Charlie would buy and sell different currencies. Sometimes a market anomaly existed whereby you could buy, say US dollars cheaper with Euros than you could with pounds and so you set up what is known as an arbitrage position to buy at the cheaper price and sell at the more expensive one. Denis continued to work all hours producing research notes on companies, commodities and economies, for Charlie to action and by the time Christmas had arrived they were well in credit in all markets.

It was a couple of days before Christmas when Charlie and Denis decided to 'unwind' all of their positions in advance of the bank holidays and also to give themselves a chance to 'draw their breath' as Denis put it, "we've been flat out for the past couple of weeks and I think we need a rest and perhaps get back to it in the New Year now unless anything major crops up between Christmas and New Year."

"OK," said Charlie, "it has been a bit intense but I'm pleased with the progress we've made. What yer doin' for Christmas then?"

Denis looked a bit depressed and said, "do you know I don't really have anyone to spend it with except you. How sad is that? Lucy and that arsehole, psychedelic Sid, are abroad somewhere and I haven't seen my kids for a few years now and it's not like they think I'm Father Christmas anymore and so I think I'm stuck here with you."

"Well, I got nowhere else to go, my missus, Celeste, has well and truly bolted and there's literally no one from my old life that would have anything to do with me now anyway. Celeste didn't want children 'just yet' she kept saying and I don't think she'll ever have any," said Charlie rather sombrely.

"You know what I think we should do on Christmas Day?" said Denis.

"What?" asked Charlie

"Take a Christmas dinner for everyone down at the Shelter!"

"What?" said Charlie again, "you must be kidding."

"Look, we've fallen on our feet here haven't we? said Denis, "I mean we haven't got enough money to retire on yet, of course, but we've made a really good start and if it carries on this way, well, who knows? This time next year, as they say, we could really be 'sitting pretty'."

Charlie thought for a moment and said, "I dunno Denis. I never really got on that well with them there did I? I think I'm a bit better now that I've come to terms with things a bit more, and I have definitely learned my lessons about how to treat people – whoever they are."

"Believe you me Charlie, they will be only too grateful for anything. We could buy a few turkeys and all the trimmings for their Christmas dinner and you and I could dress up as Santa's and take in some presents for everyone," said Denis. "It doesn't have to be that expensive, a pair of socks, jumpers, underwear that sort of thing. If we get about three dozen of everything then there should be enough to go round – what'd yer say?"

"OK," said Charlie, "let's do it. You'd better phone Tom and let him know about the dinner stuff because they'll probably need that delivered there by Christmas Eve."

CHAPTER 21
Giving Back

Charlie and Denis went back to the Shelter and saw Tom. They needed help getting all of the bags out of the taxi. There were turkeys and pork joints with the usual accompaniments of pigs in blankets and stuffing together with the vegetables, sprouts, of course, and carrots, potatoes and peas. Charlie had asked Denis if they needed to provide a vegetarian option and Denis had replied that when people are on the street they will eat anything and usually cannot afford to be fussy eaters in any way and so if they are to survive they have to give up any moral obligations and eat what they are given. He went onto say that there were enough vegetables if there was anyone who was still a vegetarian.

Tom was beside himself. He kept hopping, excitedly, from foot to foot saying, "God Bless you" every time he opened another bag. "You will, of course, join us tomorrow, won't you," he kept saying to Denis and Charlie and Denis replied that they would both be there by lunchtime.

Charlie and Denis felt pretty good about what they were doing as they came away from the Shelter. Denis was particularly glad that he had the opportunity to give back to the Shelter which had helped him out on more than one occasion. He thought back to his time on the streets and although they were hard times he was surprised when he thought of those times in an almost nostalgic way. He and Charlie had also made fairly big donations, as well, which they gave to Tom and he was so grateful that it almost bought tears to his eyes.

Denis said to Charlie, "you know Charlie, in a way I miss those old days when I was on the street in a funny sort of way. I mean it was hard but you learn how to survive and I met some decent people who, like me had fallen on hard times through no fault of their own really. There was a sort of camaraderie amongst us and of course there weren't as many on the streets then as there are now."

Charlie just shrugged and said, "Nostalgia ain't what it used to be."

Denis smiled and said, "yeah, it's easy now to look back on those days through rose tinted glasses but it's also easy to forget all the cold and the hunger and the abuse. There's no way I would want to go back to that again."

"Me neither," said Charlie, "a week was enough for me. Talk about short, sharp shocks. It certainly shook me up I can tell you."

Denis and Charlie finished their Christmas shopping during Christmas Eve and managed to pick up quite a few bargains as last-minute Christmas shoppers can just before the shops close.

They went to the pub on the night and had a Christmas Dinner and several pints of beer followed by a few whiskies to finish off.

The next morning both woke with really bad hangovers that took several cups of coffee to clear. They had really not had time to get a Christmas Tree or any other decorations but they'd bought some food for a substantial Christmas Day breakfast. As they would be helping serve up the dinner at the Shelter neither of them thought they were likely to get much to eat lunchtime. Not that that bothered them as they had been well fed over the past couple of weeks catching up with all of the missed meals.

Denis gave Charlie a Christmas present which was in a shop bag as he hadn't had chance to wrap it properly and what surprised Denis was that Charlie had got him something as well. After breakfast they both opened their presents only to find that both had bought each other a watch. Both were fairly expensive brands and Denis and Charlie laughed at each other having the same idea.

"Well, neither of us have got watches after they were taken off us and we've both worked hard to get a bit of money together. So it's right we celebrate Christmas with something like this," said Charlie.

"Thanks Charlie," said Denis, "much appreciated. Now we better get a move on we're due at the Shelter in half hour."

They donned their Farther Christmas outfits which they managed to hire at the last minute on Christmas Eve and the taxi that they had booked arrived bang on time. So they were at the Shelter well in time to help with the dinner and distribute the presents.

Tom was over the moon and again had a tear in his eye when he said, "I really don't know how to thank you enough for all what you've done for these poor souls. This is the best Christmas some of them will have had for many years."

"Don't forget," said Denis, "this time last year, I was one of these poor souls that you kindly looked after, Tom. At least I'm able to show how much I appreciated it by giving something back."

Tom said, "well, you've repaid that kindness many times over today so thank you again."

The dinner was all eaten up very quickly and there were no leftovers but as there were plenty of mince pies, nuts and crisps and the like the residents could eat all afternoon. Charlie and Denis had brought in some bottles of beer and a few bottles of sherry, wine and such like. Alcohol wasn't usually allowed but they'd managed to smuggle it in and Tom had turned a blind eye to it all - after all it was Christmas!

Tom had arranged for some songs to be played on an old CD player and by the end of the afternoon a fairly vigorous singsong was on the go. As the CDs were old most people seemed to know the words and Charlie remarked to Denis that many people can't remember what they were doing a week or so ago and yet they could remember every word to a song released well over forty years ago.

"One of life's great mysteries," Denis was saying when Dobby Bobby and Leddy Eddie came up to him to thank him for all the stuff he'd bought.

"It wasn't only me but, Charlie as well who wanted to do this," said Denis and Bobby and Eddie thanked Charlie as well and said that he wasn't such a bad bloke after all. Both of them agreed that it was the best Christmas either of them could remember for a long time.

Denis said, "I'm glad you're better Eddie, Bobby told us you were in hospital a little while ago, you OK now?"

Eddie was a huge bloke at least six feet tall although a little stooped over now as he must have been getting on for at least sixty years of age. It looked like he would have weighed well over 17 stone at one time, because the clothes he was wearing hung lose on him, although he still looked to be a big bloke.

Bobby on the other hand was on the small side and had a sort of furtive, rodent like look about him because he'd spent so long on the street now that he was constantly vigilant.

They'd both cleaned themselves up but said they were saving the new clothes that Charlie and Denis had bought them for Christmas when they left the Shelter the day after Boxing Day.

Denis was surprised that they had been allowed to stay the three nights from Christmas Eve and Eddie explained that everyone who attends the Shelter drew numbers out of a hat and if your number came up you could stay. As a number of other places let the homeless stay over the Christmas period most of them would be put up somewhere. Because Eddie had a fair few teeth missing and with his Northern accent, it took a little while to get the gist of what he was trying to say.

"Don't mind him," Bobby said with a smile, "e's pissed e' is, it only takes one bottle and e's away."

As it got dark a few sandwiches appeared but most people were full although some managed some Christmas cake and tea or coffee. A sort of warm glow settled over the Shelter that Christmas night and most of the people there had started to nod off to sleep.

Denis and Charlie stayed till about eight and then went back to their house for a few nightcaps. They'd manged to get hold of some 12 year old single malt whisky which they put a major 'dent' in.

Next day was Boxing Day and Denis and Charlie went to a local football match followed by dinner in the pub. There was a live band on but although Charlie seemed to be enjoying it, Denis said that he couldn't hear himself think and so they went back to their house to finish off the whisky.

The day after was a Sunday and so it wasn't until the Monday that they were back at the laptops and trading once more. On reflection, they'd thought it better to do a bit between Christmas and New Year in order not to miss out on anything, and also, so that the first day after the New Year's day bank holiday they could hit the ground running.

CHAPTER 22
New Year – New Hope

Although January can be a depressing month, in many ways, there are generally more gains on the financial markets than any other month and so Charlie was straight in pushing everything to the limit. Denis was continuing with the research although it sometimes just wasn't fast enough for Charlie who would shout, "c'mon, c'mon get a move on, I need that info now not next bleedin' week!"

As the markets could move very quickly, Denis was having to put in long hours researching different companies for the buying and selling of options and for some spread betting punts. He also read very widely, and quickly, about different economies especially inflation and interest and employment rates so that they could buy and sell foreign exchange which was a market that Charlie felt had a lot of untapped potential.

Charlie said to Denis, "this arbitrage malarkey seems too good to be true but it's making us a ton of money out of this sort of thing because governments constantly think that they can outsmart the market – which they can't. They try and prop up their currencies but once the markets senses there's a few quid to be made then they don't stand much of a chance – do you remember that bloke Soros who bet against the UK currency when John Major was PM?"

"Yes, I vaguely recall something about that in the early 1990s wasn't it? replied Denis

"That's it," said Charlie, "well he was reported to have made absolute millions when the UK government tried to support the pound and of course failed."

Denis wasn't really convinced and sometimes worried about

the risks that Charlie took but he had to admit that Charlie did know what he was doing. They were well ahead and both were thinking about expansion.

It was towards the end of January that Denis said, "I think we need to sort out some office space and some help, don't you? We can't keep on like this, burning the candle at both ends, and it's starting to take its toll. After all neither of us are getting any younger."

"You speak for yourself, Denis, I'm still in my prime, I am. But I must admit that I could do with some help, in fact, it can't come soon enough for me Denis," Charlie agreed, "why don't you get in touch with some estate agents that have some commercial properties on their books. I think we should also think about each of us buying a house now that we're taking off. We should tuck some of all this money that we're making away in properties and I'm sure Malcolm will help out with any mortgages we need as well."

Denis said, "yeah, I think I'll get in touch with the Judge anyway to see how things are at his end. We've made a lot of money very quickly and I don't want him getting any wrong ideas."

The following day Denis made appointments with a couple of estate agents to see some offices near where they were. He also placed an advert for staff in the local and trade papers. Charlie and Denis had decided to recruit direct rather than going through an agency because they knew exactly what they were looking for. What they weren't prepared for was the avalanche of applications that they received. These came in by post, by email and through the company web site.

Charlie carried on doing what he was good at - making money. He seemed to have a sixth sense and even when Denis provided detailed statistics he still sometimes went with his gut instinct, rather than the stats, and invariably it proved right. Not all of the time, of course, but enough for them to beat the odds of random chance. So Charlie naturally thought he had a special gift and talent and he reminded Denis of this whenever he had the opportunity. Denis thought some things never change.

Meanwhile, Denis had been in touch with Malcolm and had arranged to meet him in the pub as usual. He said to Charlie, "I'm meeting the Judge… Malcolm in the pub tonight, do you want to come?"

"Can't," said Charlie, "I got some American call options that I've got to keep an eye on and one or two other punts in the American markets and so I'll need to keep on the ball tonight. Probably be an all-nighter again for me and so keep the noise down when you come in."

Denis thought Charlie's really adapted to this new role of trader and he's certainly got a flair for it. He's bringing in tons of money and that reminded him to ask Malcolm about the house mortgages when he saw him.

In the pub later that evening, Denis said to Malcolm, "is it too late to wish you a Happy New Year?"

"It is a bit Denis," said Malcolm, "I mean we're nearly in February."

Denis laughed and said, "doesn't time fly? So how have you been Jud…. Malcolm. Been keeping your nose clean. Still working on a long scam at the bank…"

"Now wait a minute Denis, I didn't come here to be insulted by you. You know I'm legit these days and as it happens I've just been promoted at the bank!"

"Well good for you Malcolm, well done, and I mean that. I was just winding you up about scams. Now that you've made it back into the mainstream the last thing you want to do is to risk it and end up back on the streets again."

Malcolm said, "too right Denis. I don't think I could face that again, could you?"

Denis thought for a moment and said, "I think I'm looking back through rose tinted glasses these days because I was saying to Charlie the other day that I was a bit nostalgic for the old days when I first ended up on the Street. But, no, I wouldn't want to be back in that situation again."

"Well, you wouldn't catch me wishing those days on anyone. I don't think I'll ever get over the cold and the hunger. God Bless Tom and that Shelter he runs. I think both you and I would have gone under, long before now, without it."

Denis smiled and said, "yeah, I guess you're right. It would be no fun being on the streets in this weather we're having."

Malcolm replied, "these storms that we get these days, they give 'em names you know now, but it don't make them any better does it? I mean it might sound like a nice name but it can howl up a right gale and piss it down for days on end. No I don't think we'd want to be out in this."

Denis got the drinks in and they both went for the pie and chips and settled in a booth to eat their dinner.

Malcolm asked how Charlie was and how the business was going. He said, "there seems to be a large surplus hitting the savings account regularly? I set up the 'sweeper' facility from the business current account so that the surpluses could be deposited overnight as you asked."

Denis replied, "we're making a go of it Malcolm. Charlie's putting in long hours and a lot of effort. Well we both are to be fair. I do my bit which tends to be research and admin. But Charlie definitely has a flair for the business. Which he reminds me about whenever he gets the chance."

"That's good to know that you're making a go of it," said Malcolm, "and so do what do I owe the pleasure of this meeting with you Denis, what are you after?"

Denis protested, "can't a bloke have a drink and a bit of dinner with one of his mates without there being and ulterior motive?"

"Not in your case Denis, no," replied Malcolm, "come on, out with it, what is it that you're after now?"

Denis said, "well, as it happens, I do need you to see about getting a couple of mortgages for me and Charlie to buy houses with. We'll obviously have substantial deposits and so the bank will have the security it needs. There's no real risk on your part."

"You've only been trading for a little while and so there is a real risk isn't there?" Malcolm went on, "if you can put down at least 20% or so deposit then maybe I'll look at it."

"Don't give me that, you know as well as I do so long as there's enough value to cover the mortgage, and we pass the affordability criteria, you'll advance us the money. And you know you are going to convince your lending panel that we can afford it, aren't you?" said Denis.

Malcolm looked at Denis for a while before he spoke, "OK, just this once, I'll back you but don't make a habit of thinking you can steamroller me into doing anything you like especially when it comes to you borrowing money. The bank will still need a significant deposit from you both"

Denis started to say, "Malcolm would we....." when they were interrupted by a woman about the same age as Denis and what can only be described as being well preserved. Denis looked at her enquiringly as she said, "I thought that was you."

Denis was racking his brains trying to recall the woman who he was sure he'd never met before when Malcolm said, "Oh hello sis, this is Denis a friend of mine from way back. Denis this is my sister, Monica."

"How do you do?" said Monica.

"I'm fine, how are things with you?" said Denis as he looked at Malcolm and continued, "you never told me you had a sister Malcolm. In fact you kept that very quiet."

Monica looked at Malcolm and said in a joking fashion, "you're not ashamed of me are you, Malcolm?"

"Oh, nothing like that, it's just that the topic of family never really came up. When I first met Denis that sort of thing wasn't really talked about, was it Denis?"

Denis looked at Monica and said, "I suppose not. When I first met your brother we were both on the streets and you don't talk about family and that. What do you do for a living Monica?" he enquired.

Monica had an amused look about her as she replied, "I do volunteer work at a local charity."

"Very noble and which charity is that?" asked Denis.

"I work for the homeless charity, you must had heard of it, it provides shelter for people living on the streets," replied Monica.

Denis looked at Malcolm and Malcolm just returned Denis's stare. Monica, reading their minds it seemed, said, "yes, that's right, Malcolm was on the street and that's when I got involved with the charity. A few things have moved on since then of course but I'm still happy to do a few days each week, helping where I can."

Denis mumbled something about it being very worthwhile as Monica said that she would see Malcolm soon and she added, "I hope I bump into you again sometime Denis."

"Me too," said Denis as she waved goodbye to them.

Denis said, "you're a dark horse, you are, Malcolm you kept that quiet. But I don't remember seeing Monica about when I was on the streets though considering she works with the homeless."

"No, it was only after she'd helped me get straight that she started to volunteer and I think you'd moved on to one of your temporary jobs at that stage. Well she got me straight and decided to volunteer to help others. Cost her her marriage though.

Her husband was a bit of an arsehole and he didn't like her spending her time with the homeless. 'Bums' he used to call them and it just got a bit too much. He laid down an ultimatum, them or me and basically she chose them."

"Hmm," said Denis almost to himself, "a fine-looking woman."

CHAPTER 23
Estate Agent Blues

Denis met the first lot of estate agents at some offices converted from what looked like old guest houses. After half hour of the usual bullshit Denis had had enough and said, "this is just not suitable, don't you have anything else?"

The estate agents, being what they are, prevaricated and intimated that they did have other commercial properties on their books but that it was a lot more expensive. Denis politely told them where to go and saw the next lot of agents the following day.

They showed Denis some offices which weren't very modern but which could be smartened up and once redecorated he felt sure that they would be fine. There was one main office area, two private offices with adjoining areas and a large meeting room plus a smaller meeting room. Absolutely ideal thought Denis.

When it came to negotiating the lease payments Denis said that it wasn't really what they had in mind and the offices would need extensive redecoration and offered 50% of the asking rent. The estate agent said he might be able to get 20% off but didn't think the landlord would go lower. So Denis agreed that if they could get a substantial discount on the initial rent then they would go ahead from the beginning of February.

Denis thought these estate agents should wear highwayman masks when they robbed you. They really were only interested in their commissions. The estate agents pointed out that February was only a couple of days away and that they would have to 'pull out all the stops' to get the rental agreement sorted out by then. Denis suggested that they get a bit of move on then in order to earn their commission for once.

Denis met up with Charlie later that day to let him know that everything was progressing including the house mortgages. Denis said that Charlie would have to find time to view some houses and Charlie just said that he couldn't spare any time at the moment as he was at a critical point in some deals.

Denis said, "Well I'll go ahead and have a look at some houses for me and get that underway and then you can have a look once we've moved into the new offices and got you some help."

"That's fine with me Denis," said Charlie, "I'd like to get the business set up in these offices you've got lined up first – they sound ideal for our purposes. Once we're in we need a business strategy meeting because I don't want to be trading all the while. I think we should diversify into other areas as well. I know we'll get some additional help to do the trading and I'm really better at running the businesses than trading derivatives and securities."

"OK," said Denis, "we'll get set up first and then look at the direction the business is to go in."

Charlie nodded and said, "we'll need to sort out the new staff. Have you seen the number of applicants in respect of the jobs we advertised?"

Denis said that he knew there'd been a few but when Charlie said that there were literally three mailbags full, and that his email account was jammed solid and also that the web site had crashed because of all the applications all Denis could do was mumble about economic uncertainty, recessions and redundancies. He went on, "I'll have an initial trawl through first of all, Charlie, and then we'll have to select a few for interview. We'll both have to do the interviews and perhaps we can do that in the new offices."

"Yeah, that's fine Denis," said Charlie, "just let me know in good time. This trading lark is like being on a treadmill, you daren't

relax otherwise your positions can go 'belly up' literally overnight. It's bit like hanging onto a tiger by its tail."

Charlie kept beavering away and making good money, whilst
Denis dealt with the estate agents, the offices and their redecoration, moving in and his own house purchase.

This took a couple of weeks or so but everything was progressing well, Charlie and Denis had managed to sift through the applications and after studying so many CV's that could only be
described as complete works of fiction they'd managed to short
list those they intended to interview. Denis said, "I've not seen
such creative writing since I was trying to claim benefits when I
was first made homeless."

The final negotiations with the estate agents went as well as
could be expected and although they initially weren't too enthusiastic about the changes and redecorations to the offices,
that Denis had indicated, in the end they capitulated and agreed
to them. A lot of 'horse trading' had to take place because every
time Denis mentioned the changes ChasDen would be making
the estate agents wanted to charge fees. Denis was getting frustrated but concluded that the only requirement to be an estate
agent is to have a single figure IQ and continued to negotiate in
order to secure the best deal he could.

Eventually it was done and they could move into the offices.
The broadband communications had been set up and several
subscription business news feeds had been connected included
Bloomberg's and Reuters.

Denis sorted out the furniture for the offices, from a sale of
bankrupt stock, and they were able to move in fairly quickly.
Charlie followed along later and moved into his new office over
one of the weekends when things were a bit quiet. Denis said,
"well how do you like it Charlie?"

Charlie replied, "it'll do for now Denis, but the way we're doing business we may well need to expand and move again before too long."

"Business is really booming eh?" said Denis.

Charlie looked tired and said, "I can't keep this level of pressure up much longer on my own. We've done very well indeed but I'm working all hours and if I carry on like this I'll be burned out before too much longer."

"We've arranged the interviews for next week and hopefully we'll get the help you need within a couple of weeks. We'll try and get them to start as early as we can," said Denis.

CHAPTER 24
The Interviews

They'd decided to recruit two technical staff, two PA's/admin staff and a trainee trader who could provide back up to the two technical traders. Two days were set aside for interviewing the traders and a further day for the PA's and the trainee. The technical questions were to be asked by Charlie and Denis would deal with 'housekeeping' and admin. Denis felt that they should also include some personnel/HR type questions to assess character although Charlie wasn't convinced that this would do any good. After all Charlie required particular 'barrow boy' types that in his words, 'didn't give a monkey's' about how they got on well with other people provided that they got the results that Charlie wanted. Denis was a bit sceptical as ChasDen seemed to be moving away from its business ethos and seemed to be just about making money at any cost these days.

The first person in was a woman of a certain age not exactly attired for a serious professional interview. Charlie asked her several technical questions which she seemed quite capable of answering and then Denis asked her some more general questions.

Denis asked, "tell us about your strengths and weaknesses."

The woman replied that she was loyal, hardworking and honest. The usual strengths that people tend to refer to. When she was pushed on her weaknesses all she said was, "cream cakes" which had both Charlie and Denis laughing.

A couple of right 'hooray Henry's' were seen next. Quite capable but with awful attitudes which Charlie didn't seemed to mind but which Denis drew a line about.

Another young man was interviewed during the lunch time on that first day. He was very impressive both from a technical and personal viewpoint. Denis wanted to offer him the job but Charlie said that there were still several more people to see.

So it continued into the afternoon and the next day. Some very capable people were seen but most did not satisfy Denis's character requirements.

One man they interviewed seemed to be technically quite sound but when Denis asked about his hobbies which he'd put on his CV the man was a bit evasive. Denis said, "you've put here that you like painting. Is it oils or watercolours you like?"

The man pondered for a moment before responding "gloss".

Denis said, "so you mean DIY then?"

"Yeah, I suppose so" said the ex-candidate in a dopey sort of way.

However by the end of the second day they had narrowed it down to three people. The woman they had first seen and two men, one from each day.

Denis said, "I think that woman will make the best of the job, what was her name again?"

Charlie said, "yeah, I think you're right. Her name is Carol Harrison and I'm sure she'll do a good job."

"Now as which of the two blokes to choose?" said Denis.

"I think we should take them both on. They're both as good as each other and will do a good job and we introduce a bit of competition between them all." Charlie went on, "we've got enough room in the office and we can afford all three traders and, of course, each one of them should make some real money for us and so having the three will be good for business."

Denis nodded and said, "OK Charlie, you know their technical ability and they all seemed reasonably 'normal' even though some of the outfits they wore were a bit different to my day."

"All suit and ties in your day, Denis," said Charlie, "it's a bit different now and not so dependent on appearances."

"I know that, it's just that some of them we've seen are weird, what you might call departures from the evolutionary mainstream. But so long as these three can do their jobs we're all sorted then," said Denis, "just tomorrow now to interview for PA's for me and you and a trainee if you still want one?"

Charlie said, "yeah, we still need the trainee to help with the admin and keeping records of all of the trades made."

So the following day there were one man and one woman to interview for the trainee job and half a dozen, all women, to see for the two PA positions.

The first person was a young man who was quite nervous. Denis tried to put him at ease but it was difficult to interview him because he just answered any questions with the minimum response and trying to get him to expand on what he'd been doing since leaving school proved difficult.

What sealed his fate when he said that five out of three people didn't understand fractions. Denis and Charlie just about stopped themselves laughing and needless to say he didn't get the job which left the field open for the young lady who was very impressive. She had had a couple of jobs in retail but wanted to train for a professional career in finance. She had enrolled at night school and seemed to know quite a bit for a potential trainee. Charlie offered her the job on the spot and Denis was quite happy with this.

The PAs proved more difficult to fill. Many of the applicants were already in similar roles and trying to establish why they wanted to leave their current positions proved to be a bit elusive.

There were a couple of 'non-starters' who seemed to be in a bit of a dream world. Denis referred to one of them after the interview as 'Dolly Day Dream' and Charlie said of the other one that if you gave her a penny for her thoughts, you'd get change!

At the end of the afternoon they did have the two candidates who they thought would be suitable. Both were asking more than they thought they would pay but they both agreed that it was better to pay a bit more and get the right people for the jobs than to keep on interviewing which they'd just about had enough of for the time being.

By the end of the week the offer letters and contracts of employment had been sent and all of those offered had accepted the jobs with all of them being able to start during March.

CHAPTER 25
Business is booming

After the staff had all been sorted, Denis turned to Charlie and said, "we did say that we would talk more about the business model and our strategy."

Charlie replied, "I need to get back to my trades, Denis, I've lost the best part of three days and I can't afford to neglect them any more at the moment. Let's meet one of the days next week before the new staff start."

"OK, Charlie, that's fine," said Denis, "I'm going to sort out my house purchase and mortgage then over the next couple of days then if that's OK with you?"

"Go for it," said Charlie, "get yours sorted and then once the staff have settled in, then I'll see what I can sort out."

Denis wasn't relishing the thought of dealing with estate agents again but thought it was necessary to get something that he really wanted. He hadn't got a lot of time and needed to get back to the business for when the new staff started.

He was shown around several different properties not too far from the office and which were a little bit above what he wanted to pay. He reasoned that Malcolm would just have to stump up a bit more on the mortgage and then he'd be able to get what he wanted.

He settled on a nice big five bedroomed detached house with a two-car garage and extensive gardens. Although this meant that he would have to employ possibly cleaners, housekeeper and gardener he liked the place so much that he put down an offer straightaway.

Denis was on the phone to Malcolm to let him know as soon as his offer was accepted. Denis was saying he could put down a substantial deposit but would need to borrow at least £1 million. Malcolm said that he would start the wheels in motion and that there shouldn't be any problems.

So another piece of the 'back in the high life' puzzle was falling into place and the following week Denis and Charlie did indeed have their business strategy meeting.

"We need to establish what business are we going to be in over the long term," said Denis.

Charlie said, "well at the moment it's all a bit 'hand to mouth'. We're making good money with your research and my trades and we're actually cleaning up. But I'm not sure how sustainable it's going to be. We've been very lucky up till now but we've both had to work really hard to get some money behind us. It's going to take a lot more serious money to get us back to where we both used to be before we became homeless."

Denis asked, "now we have the new staff and business premises to trade out of we should be able to ratchet up the earnings shouldn't we?"

"Yes, in theory we should, but it's not quite as straightforward as that," Charlie replied. "We've been lucky and we need the new staff to be lucky as well and, it's a bit like playing a casino, you can't be lucky all the time. So we are likely to face losses every now and again. Hopefully not too many but we are playing the percentages regarding risks and sometimes they don't come off."

"We've got enough of a cushion now though, haven't we?" asked Denis.

"We have Denis, but it doesn't take much to wipe that out. A few bad trades and we could be struggling," said Charlie not really revealing how much was 'at risk' as it were.

Denis was thinking that he didn't like the sound of that and asked Charlie, "well, what should we do?"

Charlie got up and walked around the meeting room that they were in. He went up to the 'Smartboard' that was there to write out some thoughts. The Smartboard enabled a print of what was on it and so Charlie wrote up about the existing business and potential new businesses that they could go into.

It wasn't a very long list and under each of the headings Charlie started to write the pros and the cons of each business.

The first heading was to continue trading which they both thought was essential but keeping in mind potential losses they needed to diversify as well. So the next heading was about creating investment funds for themselves and others. Denis was a bit uneasy about this and said, "isn't that how you got into trouble last time by being a bit too creative with investment funds?"

Charlie replied, "yes it was Denis, but I was creating the funds just to generate business for FinCo. I was just after my bonuses and I didn't really give any thought to the long-term sustainability of the funds."

"Do you think you could create and operate investment funds that make money over the longer term and perhaps be a more ethical about it? asked Denis.

"If you're asking, again, have I learned my lesson, then the answers yes I have," said Charlie. "I think I can do the job properly now and genuinely add value to a diverse investment fund that will produce solid returns over a long term. These will be the type of funds that ChasDen will also be investing in and so I've got to get this right!"

Denis said, "OK then Charlie, if you're sure, then let's do it. What do we need to do to get it started?"

"Not a lot really," replied Charlie, "we already invest in stocks and shares as well as all the derivatives and so when we've got a tidy bit of profit to bank we start off the fund or funds depending what we can line up. Separate bank accounts and a number of subsidiaries of ChasDen will be needed to manage the funds. Once the fund starts to show some good returns and reaches a certain size we can offer it to others. By invite only though, not the catch all methods that I used to use at FinCo."

"Then let's start that straightaway, but listen Charlie, no rigging the returns this time, they have to be genuine, right? I'll get in touch with Malcom about the separate bank accounts and I'll register the subsidiaries we need with Companies House." said Denis.

Charlie nodded and said, "you have my word, Denis, that it will all be above board. Now this next one," Charlie said, pointing at the third heading on the list, "is a bit more tricky and basically means using some of the additional subsidiaries in order to create private equity funds and also hedge funds."

Denis frowned and said, "I'm not sure I like the sound of that one Charlie. I mean private equity hasn't had a good press over the past few years. Hedge funds aren't much better. I mean they don't add any value and just exploit weaknesses in the market. As I understand it a private equity fund typically buys an ailing company on the basis that they can 'turn it around'. They then proceed to sack half the staff and load the company up with a pile of debt and then they float it back on the market to get their money back together with a substantial profit! Don't get me started on the hedge funds that have virtually drive businesses to the wall."

"A number of private equity firms do operate the way you suggest, particularly the American ones," Charlie explained, "but there's no reason why we couldn't do a better job than that. You've run companies before, as well as me. Generally it's lazy or incompetent management that have brought the company to its knees. All we have to do is spot the ones with the potential to be turned around. We put in a successful management team, make it more efficient, sort out the finances and the company should then be ready to float on an exchange again."

"I'm not so sure Charlie," Denis was saying, "it sounds a lot easier than it is. It can take quite some time to turn a company around you know and what about the hedge funds you mentioned, they're not very well regarded either, as well as being risky."

Charlie smiled and said, "the thing is Denis we haven't got to buy or sell anything we don't want to. The ChasDen subsidiaries could keep a number of companies on our books, just like the old conglomerates used to do, and as for the hedge fund we would be part of a consortium."

Charlie added this point to the Smartboard and Denis thought about the possibilities. "OK Charlie, I think we could have a go at doing that as well. Provided we operate with the utmost integrity then I think it could work, both the buying and selling of companies and also running a portfolio of different companies and hedge fund investments!"

"So we are probably going to need at least three subsidiary companies to ChasDen plus the bank accounts to go with them. If we're agreed on this strategy then you're going to be busy with Malcolm setting this up."

"Charlie, we are agreed, and I have your word that you will always act with the utmost integrity?" said Denis, "I'll make a start on it as soon as my mortgage has cleared. I don't want to give Malcolm any excuse not to put that through, not that there is much an excuse he can give. After all we are expanding the business which means more fees and commissions for him and the bank as well as the odd 'sweetener' to expedite matters."

CHAPTER 26
Business Expansion from Strength to Strength

Denis's mortgage came through and he phoned Malcolm to arrange to meet him in the usual Red Lion pub once more to thank him and also to start setting up the bank accounts for the subsidiaries. He asked Malcolm how his sister, Monica, was getting on and Malcom said that he would ask her to come along to the pub later.

Although, when Denis arrived, Malcolm and Monica were already seated in the usual booth that Denis always went for, neither had a drink as they'd just arrived. So Denis got some drinks in and got hold of some dinner menus for them to have a look at. They quickly made up their minds and Denis went to place the order for three of the steak dinners. Denis thought what a change it was for a woman to order the same as the men rather than some sort of salad. Most women these days it seemed were on a perpetual diet of one sort or another. It's funny he thought but you never hear anyone saying that the could 'murder' a salad the same way you did for other meals.

Monica said that she had been meaning to get in touch with Denis, but the charity was particularly busy at the moment. The number of homeless people usually increase just after the Christmas and New Year celebrations have finished but, for some reason, this year the increase in the numbers of homeless had continued well into the year.

Denis talked about his new house and the business in general. He was saying that they were settling into the new offices when the food that they had ordered arrived. All three of them tucked in and Denis ordered a couple of bottles of wine to go with their dinner.

Denis and Monica chatted away during the meal so that Malcolm felt very much like a 'gooseberry'. But after the dinner was finished and the plates cleared, Denis said, "I need to talk about a bit of business with Malcom, Monica if you'll forgive me?"

"Don't worry about that Denis," said Monica, "do you want me to go and powder my nose or something?"

Denis replied, "I don't think there's anything that you shouldn't hear but do please keep it to yourself because it is confidential at the moment."

Malcolm was intrigued and said, "well providing you don't want any of the banks' money I'm 'all ears'," and laughed.

"Funny you should say that Malcolm," joked Denis and after a pause added, "no, only kidding. I don't think we'll need anything more than a few more bank accounts at the moment."

Malcolm jokingly mopped his brow and said, "phew, I thought you would be tapping us up for some loans now that your business is expanding."

"Not at the moment Malcolm," said Denis, "but it may well come to that in the future."

Denis went onto describe the strategy that he and Charlie had worked out and Malcolm and Monica both nodded their heads at the appropriate time and when Denis had finished they both clapped. Denis told them to be quiet and not draw attention to themselves or someone might start trying to find out what was going on.

Malcolm summarised what Denis had told them and said that he thought it was quite an ambitious strategy but that it just might work. He kept emphasising about keeping it all on the 'straight and narrow'.

Denis assured him that he and Charlie were committed to making it work and would he get the bank accounts created. Malcolm said that that wouldn't be a problem and to just let him know the names of the subsidiaries.

Malcolm then excused himself and said that he had to be somewhere else leaving Monica and Denis in the pub to finish off the wine. Denis said, "once I have my house a bit straighter I was wondering if you would like to come over for a meal one of the evenings?"

"That would be nice," said Monica, "I think the charity work should slow down a bit soon and I'll have more time. Let me give you my mobile phone number and then you can call me when your place is ready for inspection."

"I don't know if it'll pass inspection but I can promise you a decent meal. Once upon a time I used to be a reasonable cook and I'm thinking of perhaps cooking something similar to what we've had tonight if that would be OK with you?"

Monica said that sounded good and that she would bring the wine to go with it.

The rest of the evening passed in small talk and both Denis and Monica were pleasantly surprised by how much they had in common and not just the homeless.

CHAPTER 27
Onwards and Upwards

ChasDen continued to prosper throughout the year. The new staff had occupied the offices for quite a few weeks now. Denis had moved into his new house and was seeing Monica regularly and Charlie had bought a house similar to Denis's and just about a mile or so away. It was all progressing far better than Denis or Charlie could have imagined.

The trading floor of the office, if it could be called that, consisted of the three traders; Sam Smith, or Sam the Man as he liked to be known, Carol Harrison and Joe Cook, together with the trainee, Sheila White (and every time Charlie happened to be passing her desk he can't resist putting on an Australian accent and saying 'g'day Sheila, what's happening, love').

Sam the Man is in his late 20s and very full of himself. He is almost stereotype 'barrow boy' material and he and Charlie get on like a house on fire. Denis thinks Charlie sees himself in the young man or how he would have liked to think of himself when he was that age. Sam's got a rough working-class accent, swears like a trooper and is their most aggressive trader.

Joe and Carol are much calmer traders and plough on at a steady rate. They don't bring in as much money as Sam but then they don't take the sort of risks as he does which would give most people sleepless nights. Carol always dresses in a fairly flamboyant way and is what some people would describe as straight talking whilst others would just call her blunt. In her early 30s she'd done this type of work before and is very good at it. Joe struggles a bit more and is very much in Sam's shadow. He is the same age as Sam but doesn't have any of the pushiness and is perhaps too nice to be a fully successful trader.

The trainee Sheila is keen to learn. She is early 20s and gets on well with everybody in the office and clients on the phone. Working in retail has given her very good interpersonal skills. She frequently asks the traders to help her with her college work and Joe is always willing to help but Carol and Sam are usually too busy.

The office is open plan with the usual paraphernalia about the place and late this one afternoon Sam typically disturbs everyone by shouting out, "Yes!" and punching his fist in the air. Joe, Carol and Sheila all turn towards him with puzzled looks on their faces.

Sam says, "I've just made a 'killing' on the American market. I bought call options in the Tech sector and Congress have just announced massive technology investment plans for the public sector which means when I sold these options just now I made millions of dollars profit! I'm probably the best trader in the world."

The other three clapped him, although Joe muttered under his breath, that perhaps they should start calling Sam 'Carlsberg' now. There was a bell hung up at one end of the office for just such an occasion and as Sam was ringing it, Charlie came out of his office to ask what was going on. Sam said, "I've just made a killing, boss, like I said I would on those tech stock options."

"Well done Sam, very well done," said Charlie, "there should be a nice bit of bonus out of that deal for you."

"I'm looking for a lot more than a 'bit' of a bonus," said Sam, "I've just made this company millions of dollars profit and I expect a good percentage of that!"

Charlie looked at him and thought how he reminded him of himself when he was his age and just said, "well, let's see what your total position is at the end of the financial year eh?"

Sam looked a bit crestfallen and Carol secretly smiled thinking that would bring him down a peg or two. You can't just rely on one trade in this business she thought.

Joe said to Charlie, "it that the same for all of us boss?"

"Yeah, all of your performance bonuses depend on your overall positions at the end of the year as specified in your contacts of employment," replied Charlie, "now get back to it. We need a lot more results like this to get the investment funds of the ground let alone the private equity venture we will be starting."

As Charlie returned to his office he noticed Sheila and said, "g'day Sheila," which she thought incredibly funny even though she'd heard countless times by now.

"Isn't he wonderful?" she whispered to Carol in a dreamy sort of way.

Carol looked at Sheila and said, "if you like that sort of thing."

Joe wandered over to them and Sheila said, "Joe, what are these call options that Sam's just talked about? I think it's one of the topics for my college course."

Joe said, "I'll come over to your desk and go through it with you."

Sam and Carol were back on the phones making money again both thinking that their bonuses will be a lot bigger than Joe's.

Charlie's PA, Janet Chatterjee, had stood up to try and look over her screened off area which was in front of Charlie's office. Janet was very short and couldn't see over the top and so she came round into the main office. "What's going on?" she asked. Charlie replied that it was just a bit business and Janet returned to her desk. In her 40s she had been the PA to several different business. She was always discreet and confidential matters remained confidential. Very tidy and well organised and she worked to the clock because of family commitments.

Denis was out of the office again, as usual, as he seemed to constantly have meetings with the accountants and legal advisers. His PA was a lady called Elaine Knight, a 50 something year old who was quite prim and proper and did not approve of the bois-terous behaviours of Sam. Elaine remained at her desk behind her screening outside of Denis's empty office typing up notes of meetings, that Denis had attended earlier, into her computer.

There were terminal and docking stations on each desk and the office network could be accessed from home with all the usual security precautions. Now and then most of the staff took ad-vantage of working from home. They sometimes found that they could get more done without the usual distractions of working together in an office.

In addition to the office network there were dedicated ter-minals for news feeds and links to the market exchanges. There were a couple of TVs on the walls tuned to the Sky News channel and the BBC 24 hour news coverage. All in all it looked the typ-ical financial trading company set up.

CHAPTER 28
A typical day at the office

Like all offices there were certain rituals and routines that soon became the established norms. The offices of ChasDen were the same as most offices, whatever the business, there is almost a predictability about how they look. The layout was a sort of organised chaos with desks and chairs of various types, depending on who had a bad back. There were the computer terminals, docking stations and printers, the usual array of equipment, and the more aesthetically pleasing plants and screening. On the desks was the usual paraphernalia including mascots, cuddly toys, diaries and calendars, some with those sort of mottos that are supposed to make the staff feel motivated. After the bender that Sam had had the night before nothing short of an atomic bomb would have motivated him. He just sat at desk with a greenish hue to his face staring out with a sort of glassy look to his eyes.

Elaine, looking immaculate as always, was usually the first to arrive and she had been there some time before Sam turned up looking the worse for wear. Joe, Carol and Sheila all tended to arrive at about the same time just after nine a.m., although on occasions an earlier start might be required. Janet was usually last in because of taking her children to school. This was resented by Elaine who thought that all of them, regardless of personal commitments, should be in well before nine o'clock. Elaine also privately objected to the casual wear favoured by the younger ones as she was what would be termed 'old school' these days and thought that appropriate office wear should always be very smart and presentable.

Joe was smiling rather maliciously about Sam's hangover and said, "where did you get to then last night?"

Sam just groaned and shook his head.

Carol added, "you ought to be able to take it by now the amount of practice you keep telling us you have at various bars about town."

Sam looked at her with glassy, blood shot eyes and whispered, "it's not the booze as such. I've had no sleep see. I've come straight here from last night's session."

Carol just said, "a youngster like yourself – no stamina these days."

Joe said to Sheila, "hopefully we'll have a quiet day for a change with a subdued Sam the Man."

Sheila just laughed and put out her college homework on her desk.

Carol looked and said, "don't you think you should do a bit of work first before your college stuff?"

"Oh, Charlie and Denis both said that I could do homework when it was quiet," she replied.

Joe chipped in, "I meant that Sam wouldn't be shouting his head off as usual when I said it was going to be quiet not that there wouldn't be any work to do."

Sheila looked a little confused and said, "well that's not what you said! You said it would be quiet and so I've some catching up to do and can you explain those option thingies again to me?"

Carol just shook her head thinking to herself that if Sheila had another brain cell she'd be dangerous.

Joe was wondering if Sheila would ever get the hang of finance. She was pleasant enough in her own way and very enthusiastic but sometimes he wondered if the 'hamster fell asleep at the wheel' when he was trying to explain things to her.

Occasionally Janet or Elaine would come out of their cubby holes, as the screening surrounding them, were called by the others, to pass on instructions from Charlie or Denis. This particular morning Janet approached Sam to ask him to follow up on a couple of trades Charlie was interested in.

Sam said, "I can't do this today, I'm having a virtual duvet day today."

"What's that supposed to mean?" asked Janet.

"It means," interrupted Joe, "that he's not really here. He might be here in body but his not here in mind. In fact, we think he left his mind in the pub last night."

"Well why doesn't he go home then?" enquired Janet who didn't drink and thought that those that abused the stuff were a bit simple in the head.

"That's what we'll all wondering as well. He's no good here. Go home Sam, now." said Carol and turning to Janet said, "Joe and me will look at those trades, leave them with us."

So Sam went home and the day continued with Sheila doing her homework and Carol and Joe working on Charlie's trades with Janet pestering them every so often. Elaine remained aloof from all these goings on and had plenty of work that Denis had left her to do. However she still found time to, in her mind, supervise the rest of them naturally, but mistakenly, assuming that she had the superiority over them. Being the oldest she had a profound sense of loyalty to her employers something she felt was lacking in younger people.

Lunch time usually consisted of sandwiches at desks and a young couple delivered to offices in the vicinity. They usually popped into ChasDen about 11:30 in the morning and had a variety of sandwiches, cakes and snacks on offer in their wicker baskets.

The office had its own coffee filter machine which was kept on the go pretty much all day and by the end of the day nearly everyone was 'hyped-up' due to drinking too much caffeine.

The staff tended to carry on working during the lunch break although occasionally they would stop and have a bit of a chatter about what was going on in the world. Elain and Janet would join in now and again and, when they did so, the discussions invariably ended up in a rather heated debate about the attitudes of society not being as good as they were a few decades ago. Elaine quite frequently voiced her opinion that young people today had no moral fibre whatsoever and were only interested in instant fame or get rich quick schemes. Janet supported her to a certain extent but the others thought it was just rose tinted nostalgia. The discussions invariably turned back to work though because the events taking place outside in the big wide world tended to impact stocks and shares and the derivatives that they traded on a daily basis.

There was a fair amount of office banter bordering on plain insulting. Sam got the brunt of this when he was there. Carol was working on her own account more and more and Joe guessed that she was carrying out 'foreigners' for her friends, buying and selling, on the firms account which only Joe seemed aware of. But as he had his own side-line he turned a blind eye.

Sheila was too busy with her college work to notice and Janet and Elaine couldn't see all that was going on from behind their screens. So a 'greed is good' attitude started to take over.

It's difficult to say if Charlie and Denis were aware of the subtle but persistent change in the overall office morale or if they just chose to ignore it. Charlie would almost certainly condone it anyway and his promises of keeping everything transparent and on the 'up and up' seemed to have disappeared like a weak fart.

Denis should really have taken steps as soon as the 'Money God' started to take over. As soon as the only thing that people can see is how much profit is there to be had, then other things tend to go 'out of the window'.

CHAPTER 29
An office is no place to do business

As the weeks passed Sam continued to shout about his successes. It was almost impossible for him to be modest and every other word became an expletive as he became more and more excited about his end of year bonus. It was all he could think or talk about and he didn't care who he was 'stitching up' in order to make money.

Sam used a scatter gun approach and backed all of his hunches whether it was to do with forex, derivatives, CDs or spread betting Sam didn't care provided he made money. Everything was fair game and the others noticed a growing impatience whereby he wouldn't wait even a nano second for anything. He'd shout at Sheila to get people on the phone, he shout at Joe and Carol to back off from his clients if they came through on their phones when his lines were busy.

Denis thought that Sam was becoming increasingly unstable. It seemed as though he pranged his car every five minutes, his girlfriend had left him and he looked exhausted. Denis wasn't sure if Sam was using cocaine but it wouldn't have surprised him and he'd mentioned his misgivings about Sam to Charlie on several occasions now. Charlie always replied that so long as he brought in money it didn't matter. Charlie said to Denis, "he can come in stark naked whistling Dixie as far as I'm concerned just as long as he's bringing in the money!"

Joe and Sam clashed quite frequently as Sam tried to boss Joe about and he always belittled any successes Joe had. On one occasion Sam was berating Joe over a particular trade when Joe said to him, "if you can find a taxidermist willing to do the job – Get Stuffed!"

Carol and Sheila both laughed as Sam stormed out of the office. Carol said, "I've seen this sort of thing before, when money becomes the only objective then nothing else matters and everything else is right out of the window and halfway down the street."

Sheila said that she hadn't ever seen anything like it and wondered what would happen now.

"Oh he'll be back," said Carol, "if he can last the distance he should pick up a substantial bonus which should be enough to get him through rehab."

Joe looked at her said, "so you think he's using as well?"

Carol looked at him and said, "keep up, have you ever seen anyone behave like that who wasn't using?"

Joe just shook his head and the three of them went back to work.

Elaine and Janet were outside of their cubicles staring after Sam. Neither of them were very impressed with such behaviour and Elaine thought it was disgraceful. "Would never have happened in my day," she kept saying.

Charlie and Denis were in the meeting room but had heard the commotion and looked round the door just as Sam left slamming the outside door behind him.

"I don't think he's going to last much longer Charlie, I think you may have pushed him too hard." Said Denis.

Charlie shook his head and said, "no he'll be back Denis, just you wait and see. He just gets a little bit excited when he thinks about money."

Denis replied, "the problem is Charlie, that's all he thinks about."

Charlie said rather defensively, "we need that money if we're to go forward with our plans for diversification and you're happy enough to spend it on your house and the cars that you've bought."

"Charlie," said Denis, "you know I've had no more out of this business than you. You've got yourself a nice house and a couple of nice cars the same as me. That's not the point."

"Well what is the point?" Charlie said, "we need the money and Sam's making more money than the rest of us put together."

Denis was shaking his head and said, "didn't we agree that we would be more morally responsible this time round? Both you and I came unstuck because of greed. All we could see was the money. For you in particular, nothing else mattered but now we've said that other things will matter in our business and it's about time we stood up for what we believe in."

Charlie looked at Denis and said, "you didn't really believe all that crap did you? We were just talking and I suspect feeling a bit unsure about if we would ever make it again. Well we've made it now and so you can drop the pretence and concentrate on the money like what I'm doing."

"So you're going back on your word? You promised me you had changed and would do the right thing. Have you seen the effect on the others that Sam is having? He's destroyed any team spirit and brought the morale of the office to a very low level. It's worse than anything I've ever seen" Denis said.

Charlie said, "Denis, Denis, you're being far too sensitive about this. Just remember we need an awful lot of money to start the investment and hedge funds and also for a stake in a private equity business."

"What do you mean a stake in private equity, I thought we would build our own private equity set up. Manage our own funds and only work with others as part of a consortium?"

"It will take too long Denis, besides with some of the contacts I've now got we can get in quick and make even more money."

Denis sighed, "is that all it is to you Charlie, making a quick buck? We said we would set up a business for the long term that's morally good and will provide a sustainable future for us and our employees."

Charlie looked out at the main office staff and said, "they'll be alright, just you wait and see. When they start taking home more money than they imagined then all these 'niceties' of yours will be right out the window."

Denis said, "I think you should be more concerned about the way they are making this money than gratified by it."

Charlie just shrugged and thought that Denis was 'losing it' a bit.

Denis went on, "I can't think of a word to describe Sam's attitude. You know he's completely unstable at the moment, don't you?"

"Stop worrying," said Charlie, "you sound like an old woman. It'll be OK you wait and see."

"Even my subconscious realised this was taking things a bit too far," said Denis, "what happens if Sam damages himself in some way? Don't you think we have a moral duty of care to him?"

"All of this legal stuff is getting to you. Just because we said we would follow the law doesn't mean we can't bend it from time to time. These people were selected by you and me because they could do what we wanted them to do." Charlie went on and did an about turn which surprised Denis, "do you think I would just use them up and burn them out like that? If you do then you don't know me very well at all! I'm committed to running a morally sound and ethical business here and I'm hoping that the staff that we have will be with us for the long term. After all we're going to need people to run some of the diversification projects we have in mind. So Denis, please keep up with me on this and you have my assurance that I will look after everything the right way."

Charlie thought that that statement ought to satisfy Denis after all it was a potent mix of half-truths and total bollocks. Charlie was back to his old ways and had no intention of running a business in the way he'd described it to Denis. What counted was making money and loads of it. He just needed Denis off his back for now.

Charlie thought that he needed to get Denis focussed on other things and so changed the subject, "how are things progressing with the lawyers and accountants regarding the investment funds and the private equity ventures?" he asked.

Denis said that everything was progressing as planned and the first of the investment funds could be launched once ChasDen had enough to kick start it via the subsidiary.

"Good," Charlie said, "very good."

CHAPTER 30
The Investment and Hedge funds

Although they had only been trading for a few months there was sufficient surplus money for the first of the investment funds. Charlie had intimated before that you needed a number of funds so that, for example, those who were willing take higher risks in exchange for higher returns could do so. The main, 'run of the mill' fund would produce a reasonable return but would be slow growth and hopefully little risk. Whereas the investments in hedge funds would be very high risk and amounted little more than betting on share prices mainly going down.

Charlie said that he would run the first of the funds and get Carol to help him so that eventually she could take over the management of the fund. Denis agreed that this was a sensible strategy but said, "you'll need to let Sam and Joe know first because they'll want to know why you haven't chosen one of them."

Charlie said, "I make the decisions round here and if they don't like it then they can hit the road!"

"Spoken like a truly enlightened manager," said Denis, "what's happened to the Charlie who said he was going to do 'everything by the book, who would be wholly moral and ethical in the way he behaved and the way he did business?"

Charlie just said, "there's a time to be nice and a time to behave like a businessman!"

"And you think they are mutually exclusive do you?" asked Denis, "we started off this business with the best will in the world to make money, yes, but also to do the right thing. I think you've lost sight of this and are just running roughshod over anything that doesn't make you a quick buck!"

"There you go again Denis," shouted Charlie, "always criticising.

I don't see you bringing in much money. Oh, no, you're good at spending the firm's money on a load of red tape and legal niceties but you haven't brought in a penny!"

Denis was fuming, "where do you think you would be without me? I'll tell you either back in the dock, facing jail time, or homeless again like before. You sail too close to the wind and only just within the law!"

Charlie looked at Denis and realised he'd pushed him too far, "I'm sorry Denis you're right, I'll see Joe and Sam before asking Carol."

"Are you detecting a pattern here?" asked Denis. "I mean you seem to be reverting more to your old self and when I pull you up over it, you get aggressive and then agree to get back on the straight and narrow."

"I know you're right Denis," said Charlie, "and it won't happen again. You have my word on it."

Denis couldn't see that Charlie had his fingers crossed behind his back to negate such a promise. Charlie thought once the investment and hedge funds are established I won't need Denis and I can cut him loose. The business could manage without Denis now we're going places.

Denis closed Charlie's office door behind him just as Carol arrived. "Morning Carol," he said and help the door open for her. She was dressed in her usual flamboyant way and just smiled at Denis as she went into Charlie's office.

Carol was a seasoned investor and she had produced solid trading results and so Charlie didn't have to explain too much to here in respect of this part of the diversification process. He explained that initially they would launch two funds; a high risk, high return one and a 'bog standard safe' fund for, as he put it, "wimps". He added in a sarcastic way, "that'll please Denis and perhaps get him off my back."

Carol just raised her eyebrows and nodded at Charlie saying, "I can do whatever you need in this respect."

Malcolm had set up the bank accounts and the investment and hedge funds subsidiary would trade under the name ChasDenIH. Charlie had wanted to change the name of the main business to ChasDenT to represent the trading part but Denis had persuaded him that the 'dent' part had negative connotations. Nevertheless the investment fund would be ChasDenIV and the private equity venture would be ChasDenIP.

Carol listened intently to Charlie as he explained that several million pounds had been transferred into the CHasDenIH bank accounts. Partly from excess surpluses from the main trading business and partly from loans that Malcolm had arranged at the bank.

So the strategy for the standard fund was to buy stocks and shares only and keep them for capital growth and dividends. For the high-risk fund anything went provided it yielded the sort of returns that a punter couldn't get elsewhere. This is where teaming up with other hedge funds would work to their advantage. If enough of them 'shorted' a stock, then they could make big returns. Charlie said, "do try not to make too many losses, Carol, I will initially start things off but you will need to keep an eye on things on a daily basis, is that understood?"

Carol just smiled and said, "no problem, Charlie, I take it I'm going to be paid extra for this work?"

Charlie thought she was being mercenary and then realised that is exactly what he would have said. Always he thought people have to ask 'what's in it for them'. He replied to Carol, "we'll sort that out later Carol."

"I'd rather sort it out now Charlie so that we all know where we stand," said Carol with a smile.

"Oh, OK then, I'll pay you five basis points of net fund profits," said Charlie.

"Make it ten basis points and you've got a deal," Carol tried.

Charlie shook his head and said, "five gets you about £5000 per million made on top of your salary and other bonuses, and as I'm expecting big returns you'll make enough at five."

Carol reluctantly agreed and they shook hands. On the way out of his office Charlie told her not to say anything to Sam and Joe yet because he needed to talk to them about their roles in the investment funds which would be basically helping Carol and also he needed to rope them in for other hedge fund and private equity deals that would be coming up. The three of them could support the selling and buying which would help to leverage up the pressure.

CHAPTER 31
Private Equity and Beyond

Malcolm had been promoted again and was the account manager for the ChasDen Group as they were now called. They had several large loans which they had taken out as part of their fund management and private equity strategies and there were three companies under management. The investment fund had grown to several million pounds and the trading activities, especially in respect of hedge fund trading, were many millions a day. All activities were turning over good profits and it meant a constant vigilance in respect of any market idiosyncrasies.

Denis had been uneasy about expanding so quickly into these different activities, especially the private equity side of things, but Charlie had persuaded him to go along with it all. Relations were becoming strained as Charlie diverged from what they said they would do when they first started the business. Charlie was much more 'hard-nosed' than Denis and Denis frequently heard Joe and Sam saying that 'Charlie took no prisoners' which coming from them made a mass murder sound like Mother Teresa. Arguments between Charlie and Denis became much more frequent and with increasing intensity.

Together, with other private equity firms, they had put together three deals whereby they had a stake in the businesses that they had 'taken private'. Joe and Sam had been tasked with developing turn around strategies for two of the businesses and Denis was analysing the third to how best to make it profitable again.

The brief that Charlie had given Sam and Joe was to produce a report with recommendations on what it would take to make the companies that they were looking at profitable. Charlie had been quite clear by saying that nothing was off limits and that whatever was needed would be acted on even if that meant sacking most of the workforce.

Charlie had enabled ChasDen to get bigger stakes in the companies by promising to take over their pension fund deficits. This is where the value of the future pensions to be paid out is more than the value of the invested contributions made by both the individual and the company. These so called 'black holes' could spell the end of any takeover deals but Charlie had a plan.

Because Charlie had the trading facilities of ChasDen at his disposal he was able to manage the investment portfolio of the pension funds so that, 'on paper', the deficits 'disappeared' as if by magic. Charlie kept insisting that it wasn't 'sharp practice' but rather cutting-edge investment strategies although Denis wasn't convinced and was worrying more and more about the way Charlie was behaving. Charlie was hoping to trade his way out of the pension deficits before anyone realised that what he was doing was not strictly legal.

They had made so much money during the year that all three of the ChasDen Group of businesses were showing enormous profits. Big bonuses were on the cards for all of the staff and Sam, Joe and Carol had all been appointed as company directors alongside Charlie and Denis. The investment and hedge funds had both yielded good returns and a major part of the loans had been repaid. The private equity companies they had a stake in had required much more funding than they thought they would. Still, the massive redundancy programmes and complete restructuring, for the two of the companies that Sam and Joe were manging, should bring a big pay off early in the New Year.

The private equity company that Denis was managing was going nowhere much to Charlie's annoyance. He said to Denis, "what's the problem, Denis, we said we may have to make some cuts in order to save the business from disappearing all together?"

Denis said, "I can't put all of those people out of work and certainly not at this time of year."

"If you don't serve the redundancy notices now it's going to be well into the New Year before we can start turning the company round. Look at it this way; they'll have their redundancy cheques in time for Christmas and so will be able to enjoy themselves now," said Charlie.

"But that means that they'll have a pretty bleak start in the New Year," said Denis.

Charlie studied Denis for a while before he said, "just do it Denis. Get it done now."

"I just don't know if I can," said Denis.

"Let me put it this way Denis, it's either them or you," Charlie said.

Denis couldn't believe what he was hearing and said, "what'd you mean by that Charlie?"

"Simple," said Charlie, "I think the expression is, if you can't stand the heat, then get the hell out of the kitchen!"

"You trying to get rid of me Charlie?" asked Denis somewhat surprised.

"It won't only be me," said Charlie, "we've got a board of directors now or hadn't you noticed?"

Denis looked shocked and said, "but I'm a major shareholder, you can't get rid of me."

"Oh yes we can! You can be assured that Sam, Joe and Carol will all side with me on this," said Charlie, "so make your mind up now, the workers in the private equity venture or you?"

Denis stormed out of Charlie's office and bumped into his PA, Elaine, who had never seen him so angry. He shouted to her to bring in the documents for the private equity company he was managing and signed the letter to staff making over half the workforce redundant a few weeks before Christmas. He passed the letter to Elaine for her to print off the necessary number of copies and put his head in hands as she left his office.

CHAPTER 32
Christmas rolls around again

Denis couldn't believe how quickly Christmas had come around again and thought back to last Christmas at the Shelter when he and Charlie had provided the dinner and presents for the homeless. He'd asked Charlie if he would be coming back with him to the Shelter but Charlie had said that he would be too busy this year. Charlie had indicated that he and his former partner, Celeste, would be getting back together and that he would be spending Christmas with her this year.

Denis had been living with Monica for the past few months at his house although she had retained her own place for the time being. She frequently reminded him that he needed to run the ChasDen businesses in an ethical manner. He looked around now at his house and cars and reflected on the year. Had he changed back to how he was before, like Charlie, or had he managed to hang on to some sort of moral compass?

He hadn't told Monica about making all those people redundant and was dreading doing so. She was bound to ask especially as they both planned to attend the Shelter and provide food and drink and such like to those that were there this Christmas like he and Charlie had done the year before.

Monica took this very seriously as she worked for a homeless charity tirelessly all year round and she thought that Denis was doing the right thing. However when Denis told her what he'd had to do to keep his job she was disgusted and just sat in the expensively decorated lounge quietly looking at him as if he was from another planet

"How could you Denis," she eventually said, "after all the conversations we've had about helping people and especially the disadvantaged and the homeless ones? This is just a 'kick in the teeth' for them and those like them. I can't believe you could have been bought so cheaply."

Denis just shook his head and said, "I know, I know, I shouldn't have done it but Charlie put pressure on me to do it!"

"Charlie put pressure on you! Do you know how lame that sounds? You're a grown man who has contributed just as much as Charlie to the success of ChasDen and you are supposed to be equals in the business!" shouted Monica.

"I'll still be coming to the Shelter with you though," said Denis.

"To assuage your guilt I suppose?" asked Monica. "Don't think you can get round me, or put right what you've done by dishing out a few presents and providing some dinner. You can't resolve your conscience that easy."

Denis replied that he really wanted to go with her on Christmas Day and help with the dinner like he and Charlie had done the year before. Although Charlie had sort of washed his hands of it all he had nevertheless given Denis some money to help with the presents and dinners for the homeless. Charlie had also donated a cheque for a considerable amount for Tom to help run the Shelter throughout the year. Denis pointed out to Monica that it was a very generous amount but Monica again said it was just conscience money.

"Well Charlie's hoping to get back together with Celeste now and they will be spending Christmas together," said Denis, "I think they'll be going abroad somewhere for a few days and so won't be able to help at the Shelter."

Monica just shrugged and said, "she only wants to get back with him because he's got money again. She's shallow, superficial and acts like a spoiled child...."

"But other than that she's OK," butted in Denis trying to raise a bit of levity.

"Oh, you can joke about it all you like, but you know as well as I do that if Charlie hadn't have made it back like he has she would be nowhere in sight," Monica replied.

Denis said, "I know you're right Monica but don't let it come between us. I thought we were getting along really well and that you'd settled in here with me. You're not regretting moving in with me are you?"

Monica shook her head and said, "I don't know Denis, I'm saddened and shocked at what you've done and you don't seem to be the man I met when you were with Malcolm all those months ago."

"I'll make it up to you Monica, I really will," said Denis. "We'll help out at the Shelter on Christmas Day and then have Boxing Day to ourselves here and we can help Tom at the Shelter much more in the New Year, can't we?"

"Let's see how we get on over Christmas first and then I'll let you know about that. You've changed Denis and I'm sad to say not for the better." Monica went on, "all those ideals and morals seem to be taking a back seat now and Charlie has reverted to type, even you must be able to see that!"

Denis thought about his recent arguments with Charlie about how the business was being run and had to admit that Monica was right. He said, "Charlie has changed and yes I think he has reverted back to type. You know they say that power corrupts but it's not power that corrupts but money. Charlie is one of those free market capitalists, through and through, and I don't think he'll ever really change."

Monica added, "money's just another form of power I suppose, as you say. If you've got enough of it you can get most people to do almost anything you want and so I do think you're right, the more money you have the more likely it is to have a corrupting influence. Charlie's straight back to where he was a couple of years ago, knowing the price of everything and the value of nothing."

"He's worked very hard and initially I'm sure he was set on running a moral and ethical business. But as soon as morals got in the way of profit they were down the pan." Denis added, "he's not the only one who's like this though. There are very few wealthy people who have a strong moral compass. Oh they might donate large sums to charities such as yours but only if they get some recognition out of it and also off set it against tax if they can. So the principle on which the donation is made is all wrong. You must have come across this sort of thing in working for the charity?"

Monica said, "I know you're right about that Denis but our charity needs the donations whatever the motivation behind them. It's a shame that the world has changed so much in a way. If you think back to the Lever Brothers, Arthur Guinness and the chocolate makers such as Cadbury and Rowntree, they were able to combine profits, the work ethic and benevolence all in one philosophy. They looked after workers, customers and suppliers and looked for the long-term sustainability of their businesses!"

"Well unfortunately, it's all about making a quick buck these days," said Denis, "but let's not dwell on this now, we've got to deliver the presents and the turkeys and trimmings and all the vegetables and stuff for the dinners to Tom at the Shelter!"

Monica and Denis saw Tom at the Shelter who was again delighted by the all the things and food and drink that they had bought. They dropped everything off on Christmas Eve and returned on Christmas Day morning to help cook the dinners and serve them up. It seemed to Denis that many of the usual faces were there again and was shocked to see such a deterioration in quite a few of them. Dobby Bobby said that Leddy Eddie was back in hospital again and didn't joke about it just being for Christmas and so Denis knew it was serious this time. Merseyside Billy and the Brummie Bert were all there with a number of others, including Digger and Suitcase, that Denis knew and generally all of them were looking the worse for wear.

Denis said to Billy, "how have you been doing then Billy? You and Bert still knocking about together?"

"Not so good Strin......I mean Denis. It's getting hard out there and people are getting resentful. There's so many of us on the streets now. I don't think there's ever been a time like it. There must be twice as many out there now than when you were walking the streets, and of course they've all got their hands out which is why people are getting fed up."

Monica butted in, "we're doing all we can to help Billy but as you say there's so many homeless now that we can barely scratch the surface."

Billy nodded and said, "well, this is a bit of alright this dinner and the clothes that you've bought us again. I ain't arf feeling the cold these days I can tell you." As he wondered off to join the others eating their Christmas dinners.

CHAPTER 33
Another Year Just Begun

The New Year started off well enough for Charlie and the money just kept pouring in which is all that he seemed to be interested in now. Celeste had moved in with him but as she could spend it just as fast, if not faster, than he made it he found it difficult to keep on top of things in spite of the amounts he was paying himself.

It wasn't so good for Denis because after yet another acrimonious argument, Monica had decided to 'call it a day' and left him. She said that they would try and remain friends, after all, they would still run into one another as Malcolm was still her brother and she saw him quite frequently.

Denis was heartbroken. He realised that if he had stood up to Charlie and not sacked all those workers Monica might still be there with him. As Denis arrived at the office on the first working day of the year Charlie shouted to him, "Happy New Year Denis!"

Denis just said in a subdued way, "and to you," and went into his office.

Charlie looked a bit perplexed but then some of the other staff arrived and he wished each of them happy new years as well.

Charlie took Carol on one side and said, "how are the opening positions looking Carol?"

"Give us a chance to get me coat off," Carol replied. "As far as I know it's all pretty much as we left it before the holidays. Nothing much usually happens between Christmas and New Year."

Charlie looked at her shaking his head and said, "we nearly got caught out last year which is why I carried on trading between

Christmas and New Year. So we've got some catching up to do. This year we'll be having some really challenging targets for you all and so you need to hit the ground running."

"Don't worry," said Carol, "we've joined up with other hedge funds to create consortiums to 'short' a couple of stocks that are currently 'in play' and we are doing this on a massive scale. I wouldn't be at all surprised if these firms don't go 'belly up' and so if we can't make money out of this set up then we shouldn't be in the investment business at all."

"OK," said Charlie, "just so long as you know we want mega returns this year."

Charlie then asked for Sam and Joe to give him updates in respect of the firms they were managing in conjunction with ChasDen's private equity partners.

All three of the companies acquired through the private equity schemes they set up were now all saddled with an eye watering amount of debt. "it's a good job interest rates are so low," said Joe, "there's no way my company could survive otherwise."

"That doesn't matter," explained Charlie, "provided we can get some tame merchant bank to take on the float we're in the clear. The fact that the company may go 'to the wall' afterwards is not our concern. We just need to sell the company and look for the next opportunity!"

Joe said, "well we've done everything we can to make it more profitable, at least in the short term. Over 60% of the staff have been sacked and a new management teams appointed. They're all hard-nosed business people who have impressive CV's for the prospectus for the float."

"Sam's just said the same thing to me and so we're all set to go," said Charlie

"What about Denis's company," asked Joe, "is that one ready as well?"

Charlie said, "I'm not sure, I'll have to check with Denis."

Denis didn't seem interested and just confirmed that Charlie could go ahead with the sale of all three companies via stock market flotations. He just said to Charlie, "never give a sucker an even break, eh, Charlie?"

Charlie just shrugged it off and thought there's no way that silly old sod is going to divert me from the money we'll be making this year.

A merchant bank was duly appointed to underwrite the sales and they prepared the prospectus for each business. A number of presentations to pension fund managers and the like was arranged and it was expected before the year was out that all three would be sold off which would bring in substantial windfalls for the ChasDenIP subsidiary.

Charlie called a meeting with Joe, Sam and Denis and said that now that the three companies were virtually off their hands, or soon would be, they needed to look for the next 'targets' to strip down and load up with debt ready for sale again." A bit like a money-making sausage machine," Charlie said and laughed.

Denis thought Charlie's laugh was a bit hollow, a bit like one of those sinister laughs that the bad guys use in B movies, and said, "leave me out of this Charlie. I've still got a nasty taste in my mouth from last time."

"You're just a bit over sensitive Denis that's all," said Charlie, "once you get back in the saddle, you'll be away then with the best on them. All you have to do is think of the money you'll be making."

Denis shook his head and said, "no, I won't Charlie! That's me finished with that type of operation. It's immoral and I want no part of it."

"Just because Monica left you, it doesn't mean to say it's not a good way of doing business," said Charlie, "I mean we're not boy scouts here you know. It's a dog-eat-dog world and I want to make sure our dog is bigger than anyone else's."

"It's immoral and I want out," said Denis.

Sam and Joe just sat there looking from one to the other as though it was a tennis match.

"Can you two leave us for a few minutes?" said Charlie, and as they both went out of his office he turned to Denis and said, "now what's all this about Denis. You were all for this strategy when we started out. What's changed?"

Denis replied, "you have Charlie, you've changed. I didn't agree to this ruthless let's make a buck regardless of who gets hurt along the way."

"I haven't changed a bit Denis really," said Charlie, "you just think I have. You perhaps need to have a rest from it all. Why don't you go away for a holiday for a bit? Get a new perspective on things eh?"

"No, Charlie, I'm out," Denis said, "I don't like doing business this way and I think you're sailing far too close to the wind for my liking. I'm still not sure what you're doing is entirely legal."

Charlie was angry and said, "don't talk soft of course it's legal. After all that I've done for you Denis I thought you might be more appreciative! Is this how you going repay me – by quitting? You do realise that your shares in ChasDen have to be offered to the other shareholders and that you can't just sell them on the market, don't you?"

"After what you have done for me! Have you forgotten how I got the whole thing started? How I help set it all up? How I supported you in those early days ensuring all the trades were bringing in money? Have you?" replied Denis, "you'll just have to make me an offer for my shares won't you, because I'm out!"

"The trouble with you Denis is you've got no balls. You get scared of your own shadow. You need to take risks in this game and to be quite honest, you just can't cut it!" said Charlie. "Don't get expecting anything like the true value of your shares. I haven't got the money to waste on getting rid of you."

Denis said, "so it's come to this as it. You're showing your true colours now aren't you. I thought you'd really changed when we started this business. From that arrogant, couldn't care less who got trampled underfoot, attitude to a more caring businessman. But it was just a front to get me to go along with you wasn't it?"

"Got it in one Denis," Charlie replied, "you'd won all that money on the gee gees and if I'd have left it up to you then your idea of doing business would have been a back street fish and chip shop of some sort. That's not for me Denis! I've always been destined for better things, you know that. I proved I could build a fortune up again and let's be honest you were happy enough to share in my good fortune."

Denis said, "but that's it Charlie, both of us were lucky, me on the horses and you on the market. We could have been very comfortable and looked to retire in a year or so."

"Retire, are you out of your mind?" shouted Charlie, "I could no more retire than fly to the moon. It's not just the money, it's also the 'game' the money is just how you keep score – the one with the most money when they die – wins."

"You're sick you are Charlie! What about all the people who lose their jobs on the way? All those people who end up on the streets like we were?" said Denis.

Charlie just shrugged and said nastily, "I'll let you know in a day or two what you'll get for your shares. Don't get thinking you'll get any severance settlement – you've had enough out of this business. Now I suggest you clear your office, I think I'll get Carol to move in there, after all she is managing mega bucks now alongside the hedge funds that we're now doing business with."

Denis just turned and went back to his office. He saw Janet and Elaine and told them both he was leaving and asked them to get some boxes for his office paraphernalia.

CHAPTER 34
Life in the slow lane

A couple of months after Denis had left ChasDen he was having a drink with Malcolm explaining why he'd left Charlie to it when Monica arrived. Denis was about to tell her he'd left the business when she turned around and said that she had heard on the 'grapevine' that he'd left. Denis looked at Malcolm and he said, "don't look at me, it wasn't me who told her."

Monica said to Denis, "never mind how I found out, I just did that's all. More importantly how are you keeping and what are you doing with yourself these days?"

"Nothing much really," said Denis, "I only received a fraction of what my shares were worth but it was enough to pay off my mortgage and I just kept the one car and so although I don't have a lot at least I don't have any debt."

"So how are you filling your time then?" asked Monica.

Denis said, "you remember when I told you how Charlie and me got our original stake to go into business?"

Monica thought back and said, "yes, you told me that you had a winning streak on the horses."

"That's right," said Denis, "well I try and recreate that winning streak. I sometimes stake the old timers in the bookies to see if they can come up with the same winnings that Charlie and me did."

"So, how's that going then?" laughed Monica.

Denis laughed and said, "not so good actually. Neither I, nor any of the others I've asked, can get anywhere near it."

Monica smiled and said, "why don't you come and work with

me Denis. It's only on a volunteer basis but given your time on the streets you could be invaluable and, as you know, it's really worthwhile!"

"I don't know Monica, I mean working together, after what we've been through" Denis was saying when Monica said, "just think about will you?"

"OK, now then what's everyone having? Malcolm was just telling me he's now one of the main managers at that bank he works for." said Denis as he went to get the drinks in.

"Oh, I know what you're thinking, you two – here's another one who's sold his soul," said Malcolm looking at both of them.

He went on, "although I know you have left ChasDen, no one has officially informed me, at the bank, that you are no longer a director and shareholder. If you remember that some of the more recent loans were a bit on the high side and the bank sought personal guarantees from you and Charlie, in case the firm couldn't pay at any stage? So you could be in a spot of bother if anything happens to ChasDen."

"Yeah, I remember," said Denis, "so no one has been in touch then?"

Malcolm just shook his head rather sombrely.

"That means," said Denis, "if ChasDen runs into any problems with repaying those loans then I could become personally liable alongside Charlie! But I don't personally have that sort of money and I'd be bankrupt again. I'll bet Charlie has his side of things covered though."

Malcolm said, "I'll write to Charlie and let him know, that as you are no longer a signatory of the company, I shall be removing your name from the covenants on the loan. I'll just need a letter from you so that I can quote that rather than saying that I met up with you in the pub."

"No problem," said Denis, "I really appreciate you reminding me. It's just the sort of trick Charlie would pull. Squirrel away money and bankrupt the business leaving me to pick up the re-payments whilst he has it away abroad somewhere."

Monica said, "you need to write that letter tonight. You know you can't trust Charlie and you also know that's he's very impul-sive and, I think at times, a bit on the unstable side as well."

"I wouldn't go that far but I'll pop a letter into the bank myself, tomorrow," Denis said.

Malcolm left shortly after leaving Denis and Monica to talk about the homeless and volunteering. Monica was saying that she really hoped Denis would come back to help out but Denis was far from convinced and just thought it would be too painful to return to that type of thing now that he'd split from her. He said, "well, I will give it some thought, Monica, but I'm not sure I'm ready to go back to that at the moment."

Monica said, "well, we'll leave at that for now Denis, but you know that I can be very persuasive when I put my mind to it!"

"Don't I know it," said Denis.

CHAPTER 35
A day too late and several million £'s too short

The next day as Denis walked to the bank he thought about the previous evening and the long discussions with Monica. He had decided that he would help out at the homeless charity and planned to call Monica later to let her know. He detected that there might be a way for them to get back together again as well and even if it was only a slim chance he felt he had to take it. As he walked into the bank, Malcolm came rushing over and breathlessly said, "have you heard the news Denis? ChasDen have gone bust!"

"What!" said Denis, "it can't be."

Malcolm was shuffling from foot to foot and couldn't keep still. He kept repeating over and over that it was a disaster of monumental proportions.

Denis said, "hang on a minute Malcolm, just try and calm down and tell me exactly what's happened.

"Charlie's been caught with his hand in the till, again!" Malcolm started.

"But how?" asked Denis, "I kept a tight rein on the legalities of everything that was being done and so I don't see how he could have got round that."

Malcolm said, "you obviously don't know Charlie as well as you thought you did. If you remember when the private equity venture took over those three companies all of them were showing pension fund deficits......"

"I know that," interrupted Denis, "but Charlie traded out the bad investments and made new ones and so the deficits disappeared."

"Just like that," Malcom said doing a fair impression of Tommy Cooper.

Denis said, "what are you getting at Malcolm? I checked over all of the details and the pension funds just before I left and they all looked OK to me."

Malcolm shook his head and said, "you ever hear about 'marking to market' Denis?"

"Well yes, it's where the current market value of an investment is recorded rather than the amount the investment cost in the first place," said Denis.

"Exactly!" said Malcolm, "and can you guess how those funds were valued? They certainly weren't valued at current market values."

Denis thought for a minute and said, "Oh no! He used investment cost values."

"Worse," said Malcolm, "he made up figures from inter day trading when prices can move up really quickly and then back down again before the end of the day. To all intents and purposes he just made up the figures as he went along and the fact is that those pension funds are only really worth a small proportion of the value shown on the books."

"But I saw the information independently verifying the values."

"What you saw was what Charlie wanted you to see. In effect they were just a 'blip' on the screen that had been captured as an end of period valuation. Nothing more than that," said Malcolm, "ironic really isn't it that all the other crooks of our time have raided pension fund surpluses and reduced them to virtually nothing. Here we have a situation which is completely the reverse – a pension fund surplus has been created out of thin air – talk about magicians. The valuations are not worth the paper they're written on and the true value is anybody's guess but it's a lot less than it should be that's for certain."

Denis said, "he's just a bloody crook isn't he? That's all he is and that's all he'll ever be! How could I have so short sighted not to see him for what he really is, an out and out crook!"

Malcolm always had a sort of hang dog expression and he looked even more sorrowful, "Denis, Charlie has also pocketed the fees for the pension fund trading accounts. He's took out millions of pounds in one way or another and so the company is no longer viable. You do know what this means, don't you?"

"Well I'm out of it as you know," said Denis, "here's the letter we spoke about last night."

"Sorry Denis," Malcolm said, "it's too late. It was just before midnight, last night that they declared bankruptcy. The pension fund trustees started proceedings yesterday to recover funds they believe have been stolen. As your name is still on the legal documentation, and also as you accepted personal liability, you old son are in the proverbial S.H.1.T."

Denis looked shocked and said, "isn't there anything you can do? I mean you knew before yesterday that I had left and that it was just that the paperwork hadn't been updated."

"It might have been known informally but the bank needed formal notification that you were no longer involved. I'm really sorry Denis but the bank doesn't want to be associated with any of this and so is calling in the loans. The whole 'pack of cards' is crumbling down."

"What about Charlie?" asked Denis, "have you been in touch with him?"

"Charlie's gone Denis, he left the country last night and no one knows where he's got to," said Malcolm. "We've been trying both office and mobile numbers and there's no answer for any of the numbers we have for him."

"Oh my God, I'm really in it now," Denis said as he sat down on the nearest chair. "Let me try and get hold of him," Denis said as he pressed the speed dial for Charlie's private mobile number.

There was no answer and Denis just sat there stunned. Malcolm was saying that a full investigation will be needed but Denis wasn't really listening as he realised the implications of what all this meant.

Malcolm went on, "it seems that ChasDen has been in trouble for a little while now. Probably since you left. There were no checks and balances taking place and the records seem to have been falsified to show somewhat exaggerated profits being made. Money has been leaving the business hand over fist and finding it's way into Charlie's accounts. The forensic accountants will work out exactly what's been going on but from what I can gather the investment funds not only made spectacular losses, especially the hedge fund bets, but the overall trading in derivatives was losing money at a rate of knots as well. To say there were disastrous bets via the hedge funds would be a gross understatement. All the staff have left and the offices are closed and the firm is officially in the Receivers hands now. Huge trading losses, all of the loans wiped out and being sued by the pension fund trustees meant the end of the road for Charlie and so he bailed out before it all hit the fan, leaving you, I might add, to take all the flak."

Denis was in a state of shock and looked at Malcolm saying, "I don't know what to do Malcolm, I'm in such a shock. I mean I knew Charlie was a chancer from when I first met him but I really thought he could change. He's blatantly lied to me and others and acted illegally and it looks like whatever money there may have been he's embezzled that, no doubt to live a life of luxury somewhere abroad."

"A leopard doesn't change his spots Denis. Oh he'll be facing prosecution alright but that could take some time," Malcolm said, "and I of course will speak up for you but I'm afraid that, at least, for now, you will need to hand over all your credit cards, cheque books and the keys to your house. The bank will write to you to let you know how much you owe us once we've taken any savings and sold your house and there may well be summonses for other debts from other organisations."

Denis just groaned and handed over his credit card, cheque books and keys. He'd got enough cash on him for now to find a room. Malcolm explained that his house needed to go on the market straightaway and they would employ a firm of bailiffs to remove the furniture and household equipment. His car would also need to be sold and that would be sent to the next car auction that the bank dealt with.

CHAPTER 36
It all comes tumbling down

Denis left the bank feeling helpless and ashamed. He wandered around the streets for quite some time thinking it may come back to pounding the streets once more looking for the next handout. It started raining, not that he particularly noticed but subconsciously he had been heading for Monica's flat and although she wasn't in he managed to shelter in the hallway of her block. He'd called her on his mobile phone and left a message saying he would be waiting for her.

"Oh Denis, I'm so sorry, Malcolm called me earlier and told me all about it. He said you might be heading over to see me. Come in and get dry." Monica said when she arrived.

Denis just nodded and followed her up to her flat. He took off his wet coat and sat on one of the dining room chairs. Monica placed a large glass of whisky in front of him and said, "for medicinal purposes."

Denis shrugged and downed the drink in one go and as Monica got up to get him another he said, "I just don't know what I'm going to do." He started crying and Monica found it difficult to understand what he was saying but it was on the lines of, "how could I have trusted such a person?" and "why didn't I see it coming?" together with a number of expletives.

Over and over Denis kept reproaching himself for being taken in by that 'wide boy' and 'crook' as he kept calling him.

"He's hardly a boy now Denis," said Monica, "and let's face it he is just a crook of the worst kind in effect robbing pensioners like that. I think he had us all fooled for a time. He convinced us that he could behave in an honourable way. But it was just 'all a front' with him. What's the saying? 'He's got more front than Blackpool, something like that isn't it Denis?"

Denis whispered a, "yes, something like that," but was 'miles away' thinking about how foolish he had been. In his heart of hearts he knew Charlie was a no- good liar and a cheat. The problem was Charlie could talk his way out of most things and he always sounded so convincing. Denis had kept giving him the benefit of the doubt which Charlie had exploited to the fullest extent!

"Malcolm's told me that you've lost everything," Monica was saying, "so why don't you stay here for a while until you get yourself straight?"

Denis said, "do you mean that?" It could be quite a long time before this gets resolved and I may even end up in prison if they can't locate Charlie."

"Let's take one day at a time. I know it's not you that caused all of this. Just stay here and try and get sorted whilst you work out what to do."

"OK," said Denis, "thank you, I will."

"Don't get getting any ideas mind, it's the sofa for you!"

Over the next few days and weeks, Denis stayed at Monica's flat and as she carried on her volunteering with the homeless Denis helped. It seemed that legal documentation relating to ChasDen arrived daily. There were statements from the bank and other financial organisations which meant Denis was in debt to the tune of several million pounds. But the worst was the pension fund trustees who were proceeding with criminal cases against him in the absence of Charlie.

Denis didn't know what to do and was actively seeking legal representation. But as he had no funds to pay it was difficult to convince any of the lawyers to carry out the work without being able to charge fees, what's known as a 'pro bono' basis. He'd written back to all of those who were after him for one thing or another explaining that he'd left ChasDen some months before all this had happened and that he was therefore no longer liable. This was met with derision by everyone he'd written to and so correspondence backwards and forwards continued for some time.

Monica had convinced Denis to carry on helping with the homeless charity that she worked for and Denis also went to see Tom and some of the homeless he used to associate with. Thinking it may be coming down to this for him very soon and he might as well start preparing the ground.

Denis hadn't much cash but he still had a bet every now and again on the horses to see if he build up some sort of stake, like he did with Charlie what seemed like a lifetime ago now, but was only a couple of years or so. He never really managed to re-create that winning streak he had then.

Denis had tried very hard to convince the banks, pension funds and other organisations that he wasn't responsible for their losses but as his name was still on all of the ChasDen legal documentation he was unsuccessful. He was due in court and faced both civil and criminal charges, some which carried custodial sentences. He had finally managed to secure pro bono legal representation but his lawyers had suggested that he 'come clean' and plead guilty. Denis couldn't accept this and kept saying that he was innocent and that Charlie should be the one in court and not him.

The problem, the lawyers explained, was that it was incredulous that a man as experienced as himself acted so naively as to 'beggar belief'. In other words they thought that the jury would just not believe that he was innocent. At best they would consider that he'd turned a blind eye to the goings on at ChasDen but at worst they would be almost certain to convict him on being complicit in the overall scheme of things. If he pleaded guilty he might get a suspended jail sentence if he was very lucky.

Denis explained all this to Monica one evening and Monica was absolutely stunned that Denis had allowed himself to be conned so readily. She asked him, "are you sure you weren't aware of what was going on?"

"How can you ask that?" said Denis, "you know I disagreed with the way Charlie was going about things!"

"It's one thing to disagree and another to take positive action to prevent a crime being committed. You did, after all, make all those people redundant at Charlie's say-so"

"I did all I could to prevent Charlie acting illegally! You know that I never wanted to make those people redundant!."

Monica looked at him and said, "Denis, I don't know what to think. You went along with sacking all those people just before last Christmas. Everyone is bound to think you were complicit."

"I've explained all that!" Denis said exasperated that even Monica was doubting him.

"I know you have but I found it hard to understand and I'm sure when the jury hear about this sort of thing they are going to think that you are just like Charlie, totally mercenary in your activities"

Denis said, "well if you don't believe me, I don't think I've got much chance."

"It might be best if you moved out before your trial," said Monica

"That's really going to look good isn't it? Appearing in court with no fixed address. Couldn't I stay here until the trial?" pleaded Denis.

Monica said, "well OK, but only until the trial. Whatever happens you are out of here after that."

Denis nodded and thought unless they can locate Charlie he

would likely end up in prison.

CHAPTER 37
Is the law is an ass or is justice just blind

The day of the trial came around far too quickly for Denis. His lawyers had told him to expect the worse as they had still not convinced him to plead guilty in order to get a reduced sentence.

"I am innocent of these charges!" said Denis, "surely the truth will come out?"

The lawyers just shook their heads and reminded Denis that unfortunately very often the truth has very little to do with justice.

The case was being heard at the Crown Court because of its seriousness and Denis was aware that they could impose quite sever sentences if a person was found to be guilty.

Denis was waiting in the foyer before his trial began. He was extremely nervous and was wishing that they would get a move on so that it would all be over one way or another as soon as possible.

There were a few procedural matters to be dealt with beforehand. A few of them referred to the Crown Court from the lower Magistrates Court. Generally these were matters for sentencing and it was surprising that the first of these related to a drunk and disorderly conviction. The police had informed the court that the defendant had been so drunk that he'd fallen into a puddle and was trying to 'swim' out of it when the police approached him. He immediately became aggressive and fought with the police knocking one of their helmets off. He was arrested and placed in a jail cell overnight. He appeared in the Magistrates Court alongside all the other drunk and disorderly convictions for that day. Whilst every other single drunk had pleaded guilty, when he was asked to plead he had stated, to the amusement of the court, that he had only had the one drink. The fact that it was an entire bottle of scotch didn't seem to register with him. As it was not a first offence he received six months jail sentence suspended for two years.

Another more serious case of offensive weapons being carried was heard by the judge. This involved two people chasing a third brandishing machetes over their heads and shouting that they were going to 'kill' him. The judge asked the individuals why they wanted knives like this as he held up one of the machetes which was a very menacing looking weapon about two feet long. The response was that they were required for 'peeling apples your honour' again there had been a certain amount of incredulous amusement before the judge sentenced them to serve two years in prison.

After the remaining two other minor matters were dealt with the judge recessed for ten minutes as the next case on the list, ChasDen, was due to be heard.

As Denis went through to the court he was absolutely and totally shocked to see Charlie there waiting in the dock. Denis couldn't believe it and said, "where the hell have you been?"

Charlie just shrugged and said, "somewhere where I thought there was no extradition treaty."

"You bastard!" said Denis, "you utter bastard, throwing me to the wolves like that. You deliberately set me up as the 'fall guy' in all this didn't you?"

Charlie smiled and said, "well you and your boy scout attitude to business. Always so pious! Oh, we can't do that Charlie and we can't do this. Do you think I took any notice of your bleating?"

"You could have been straight with me and we could have split the business up a long time ago."

"It's not in my nature," said Charlie, "you ought to know that by now."

"Doesn't it bother you that I'm likely to go to prison because of your underhanded dealings?"

Charlie shook his head, "no it doesn't bother me in the slightest because you're not going to prison, neither of us are."

"What makes you say that?" said Denis, "these charges seem pretty convincing to me and the facts speak for themselves. You did, in effect, embezzle millions of pounds and from pension funds at that!"

Charlie shaking his head said, "you see those two lawyers over there – the solicitor and the barrister talking to your lawyers?"

Denis nodded and Charlie went on, "they are the best team of lawyers in the land. If they can't get us off then no one can."

"But you're as guilty as sin!" said Denis, "I've just been set up and as you know full well, I'm innocent."

"Don't give me that Denis, you couldn't have not realised what was going on. No one here is going to believe that as a minimum you turned a blind eye and more than likely you were complicit. You can be so naïve sometimes."

Denis started to protest but the judge had arrived and they had to stand up and be silent until he was seated.

CHAPTER 38
What goes around comes around

The judge took his seat and the court clerk read out the charges; that the defendants did knowingly and callously defraud pension funds and mislead other investors which resulted in the loss of vast sums of money amounting to at least £20 million. This was the amount for which there was firm evidence and it was considered to be a conservative amount. The actual amount of debts owed by the two of them probably amounted to several millions of pounds more than the indictment but the evidence was less clear cut for the total amount.

Charlie and Denis had both been declared bankrupt and were asked to plead on the charges of fraud and embezzlement. Charlie just said, "guilty, your honour," whilst Denis couldn't believe it and he said, "not guilty."

There was a murmuring in court whilst the lawyers talked amongst themselves. The one barrister stood up and said, "if we could just have a few minutes to confer with our clients, your honour, I feel sure we will be able to get a unanimous plea?"

The judge agreed to a short adjournment and Denis's solicitor said to Denis, "it will be better for you if you plead guilty alongside Charlie. You are almost certainly to be convicted and if you insist on pleading innocent you could find yourself facing far more stiffer penalties than Charlie will!"

Denis protested that he was really the innocent party in all of this and the lawyer said "it doesn't matter now because you are almost certainly to be convicted because Charlie has pleaded guilty and the court will treat you not only as knowingly complicit but also devious in trying to wriggle out of your responsibilities."

"Oh, OK, then," said Denis, "but we'd better get off with a light sentence."

The barrister acting for Charlie said that both defendants now wished to plead guilty and that he would like to make a statement of mitigating circumstances on behalf of both defendants. As agreed with Denis's barrister Charlie's barrister would be acting for both of them now.

The judge accepted this as the barrister launched into what could only be described as a fairy story emphasising the riches to rags and then back again from rags to riches that Charlie had gone through. He laboured the point that Charlie had been treated very unfairly when he had been bankrupted the first time (through no fault of his own he added – Denis was incredulous) He went on to say that this had instilled in him an urgent and remorseless desire to make enough to settle his debts and payback to society in general. He had recreated the wealth and provided employment opportunities and was generally regarded as a citizen of good character. In his endeavours he admits that he may have been overzealous in pursuit of wealth but it was only his desire to do the right thing that spurred him on.

His accomplice Denis had helped Charlie get started and like Charlie had a burning ambition to get back to some sort of normal life after he'd been living rough on the streets for a few years. Denis had been homeless for some time and even though Charlie was only homeless and living rough for a short while both of them were severally mentally scarred by the experience.

So both these individuals, the barrister argued had a forceful ambition to make enough money to straighten out whatever wrongs there may have been previously. It is therefore admitted that in acting in such a manner pecuniary interest may have taken over from their more moral ambitions but this was due to being caught up into one of the most fascinating business successes this country had ever seen.

"With this in mind, your honour, we would ask that you look leniently on these defendants," concluded the barrister.

The judge said that as they had both pleaded guilty and showed contrition in respect of their wrongdoings he was prepared to act leniently towards them particularly as neither had previous convictions.

Charlie and Denis were asked to stand for sentencing as the judge began, "Charles Cooper and Denis Jackson, I acknowledge your contrition but I am mindful of the wilfulness with which your sacked people and fraudulently manipulated their pension funds. There is also the matter of insider dealing and falsifying accounts and documents. I am left with no choice therefore other than to hand you both to custodial sentences. You will both go to prison for a period of twelve months. Take them down!"

Denis started to shout but his barrister shook his head and went up to him and said, "look that's not a bad result considering you could have gone down for at least a couple of years! With good behaviour you'll be out in six months, just in time for Christmas."

"But I don't want to go to prison," wailed Denis.

Charlie said, "you've got no choice old son, and, anyway, it's not like you've got anywhere else to go from what I hear."

"what d'you mean by that!" shouted Denis.

"It's well known that you lost your house and that Monica has kicked you out and so even if you hadn't received a custodial sentence you've got nowhere to go," said Charlie rather smugly.

Denis held back his anger and said, "well you needn't look so smug, you've lost your house as well and you'll have nowhere to go. Unless Celeste has decided to stick with you this time, which I doubt very much."

"I'd rather not go into that," said Charlie.

They were led down to a waiting prison van which was to take them to their allotted places in hopefully a local prison. Not that either of them would be expecting visitors it was just that they hoped there might be people who they knew already there.

On the way out Denis's solicitor shouted to him, "that wasn't so bad was it?"

Denis just looked at him and said sarcastically, "thanks a bunch."

Charlie's barrister saw them just before they went off to explain that the judge had agreed to an open prison where most people convicted of white-collar crimes were sent to. He said to them, "it'll be a doddle and you'll be out in six months, probably less. Keep your noses clean and keep out of trouble and you'll be back before you know it!"

As they were being driven to the prison, Denis said to Charlie, "that barrister of yours was much better than the one I got you know?"

"Ah, quality always shows Denis, you might have to pay a bit more but quality always shows."

Denis said, "my barrister and solicitor were acting pro bono because I don't have any money to pay them. How come you got such a top notch barrister if you weren't able to pay him?"

"Who said I couldn't pay him?" Charlie went on, "I may be a bankrupt but if there's one thing I've learned it's that you should always pay your lawyers and accountants even if you've got no money to speak of."

"Well how did you manage that, I thought you were as broke as me?"

Charlie said, "I never said that, I said I was bankrupt but that don't mean I've not stashed a few quid away a bit like you I suspect?"

"Why do you think I had to get legal aid if I could afford to have paid a better- known barrister?" said Denis shaking his head. "I'm flat broke, I never had chance to squirrel away any money. Not like you by the sound of it. How much did you stash and where did you put it? All of my accounts were frozen the very first day the news broke so you must have known this was going to happen and made provisions beforehand?"

Charlie said, "I suppose it must be the boy scout training kicking in – always be prepared...."

"You were never in the boy scouts," Denis butted in.

"Well whatever it was I could see the writing on the wall and decided to place some of my cash 'offshore' as they say. The Cayman Islands looked nice and so I put a bit aside and went to live out there for a time. I foolishly went on a day trip to one of the other islands which is a British Crown Dependency and got nabbed that way. I don't know how they knew although I suspect Celeste had something to do with it, the bitch."

Denis said, "I thought you two were back together and getting along OK?"

"We were until things started to go 'belly up'. Celeste has always been a bit squeamish about getting her hands dirty in any way, shape or form and the thought that she might have to do something for her money was too much for her. Coupled with the fact that she thought she never be able to 'do' the season again in Britain put an end to any loyalties she had, romantically or otherwise. As soon as she heard I'd been arrested she attempted to clear out the bank accounts down there but I manged to put a block on that before I boarded the plane back to blighty. She left in a huff after selling off her jewellery and anything else of value she could get her hands on and was on the first flight home. We almost bumped into each other at Heathrow."

They shortly arrived at the open prison and were searched on arrival. All their belongings were taken from them and they were led into a big room used to indoctrinate new inmates.

There were about two dozen that had arrived that day and the prison governor delivered his usual speech about keeping their noses clean, obeying the rules and they would find that the time there wasn't so bad and, more importantly they could be out before they knew it. He went on to explain that the way the parole system works in England is that generally, provided you had a good record and stayed out trouble then they would serve no more than half their sentence which would be just six months in their case. However, any trouble and it would be the full stretch.

The prison guards took over and explained some more about the rules and regulations which on the whole seemed to be pretty lenient. About the only thing you couldn't do was walk out of the place.

Charlie and Denis were shown to their cells and as it was pretty overcrowded they had to share with at least one other prisoner. Charlie only had one other inmate in his cell but Denis had two and was a bit uncomfortable as the two in question had already been there for some time and made it clear they didn't like anyone else sharing their facilities.

CHAPTER 39
Open prison

Prison life wasn't too bad and both Charlie and Denis were encouraged to take part in various activities to help with their rehabilitation. They discovered that they were allowed to enrol in Open University courses and both signed up almost immediately. Whilst the internet was restricted they could nevertheless read the books and carry out the assignments. It was even possible to get visits from a tutor now and again as well.

Denis chose literature and the classics whereas Charlie decided on financial strategy. Denis guessed Charlie was looking for any loopholes he could exploit when he was released. There were counsellors who they could talk to and the question of employment on the outside came up from time to time. Denis hadn't got a clue what he would do but Charlie said that he intended to pick up where he left off and that this time he didn't need stake money from Denis's gambling.

Each day was pretty much the same and time seemed to drag a bit even though the end of the six months came quickly enough and their release was just around the corner.

Prison life wasn't too bad – both Denis and Charlie made some useful contacts with others who had been caught financial wheeler dealing. Charlie was over the moon about this although Denis didn't seem to think it would do him any good because there was no way he'd go back to that life.

The biggest problem was boredom although occasionally there was a bit of excitement if a prisoner tried to 'leg it'. It was usually because the parole board had refused to release them early and other pressing issues like pregnant wives that forced them to abscond so as to be present at the birth. They had to be careful though because when they got caught again they could end up in a proper prison and not the holiday camp that they viewed the open prison to be.

Denis got a job in the library which helped with his studies and Charlie did some shifts in the kitchens. He wasn't the best cook in the world but he managed to cope with it. On one occasion he put sugar in the soup instead of salt but after being threatened by nearly every inmate in the place he never made that mistake again.

As there were a number of inmates preparing for Open University (OU) exams a conference call was arranged to take place in the library. The tutors would start off a virtual meeting and the inmates would be sitting in the library ready to take notes and participate in a virtual classroom session.

Unfortunately it didn't take place because the guard who had the keys to the library had the day off and so although the room was set up no one could get in. So much for technology, Denis thought. The tutors were at the Open University centre waiting to start and they could see the inside of the library on their screens but couldn't see any one in attendance. After several phone calls which took most of the morning it was decided to abandon the session. Later that day the prison governor had to call the OU to apologise for the fact that, in spite of all of the technology, it couldn't go ahead because the person who had the keys had had the day off.

The inmates mainly consisted of those who had committed what is known as 'white collar crime' usually fraud or embezzlement of one sort or another. This tended to range from petty thefts literally caught with their 'hands in the till' to the really big swindles created within the financial markets. Such things as 'boiler rooms', which promoted basically worthless shares, to investment scams whereby people invested in non-existent assets such as real estate property which only existed on paper. The most famous one of these was when London

Bridge was sold to American investors – twice. That was some time ago now but many of the inmates held this up as the master stroke that they all aspired to carry out one day.

Most of the inmates were bankrupt as their assets had been seized on conviction and there is a saying that if a person owes the bank a million then that person has a problem, however if the person owes £100 million then it's the banks problem. Most of the inmates subscribed to this philosophy and many of them genuinely believed that they have been wrongly convicted. After all parting a 'sucker' from his money was no crime according to them.

Of course, Denis believed he been wrongly convicted and would tell anyone who would listen, at the 'drop of a hat', how he had been 'duped' like any other investor. Most inmates would nod politely and move off although one or two told him he should have been more careful and that most people would have seen it coming, especially being in business with Charlie.

Denis came across an acquaintance of his from when he was on the streets. He only knew him as Pebbles because of his glasses and he'd never got to know his real name. "What are you doing in here Pebbles?" said a surprised Denis when he came across him.

"Oh, y'know how it is," said Pebbles in a broad Geordie accent, "I did a rushed job for a client who got nicked and it led the 'busies' back to me."

"What did you do for him?" asked Denis.

"Oh, the usual, passport, driving licence, credit cards and a few other bits and pieces. Some of my best work even if I say so me-self," said Pebbles.

"So how come he got nicked?"

"He tried to buy some drugs off an undercover cop with one of the credit cards. I mean I ask you. He was on the run and about to do a 'moonlight' when he thought a bit of 'snow' would help him on his way. It did that alright, helped him right into the nick." lamented Pebbles.

Denis tried to keep a straight face and asked, "so how long have you got?"

Pebbles said, "I'm not really sure because I'd asked for other offences to be taken into account, they knew I was homeless and it's not the first time I've been nicked mind for my creative abilities. So, all in all, I thought I wipe the slate clean ready for a new start when I get out."

"I must admit Pebbles, that you are one of the best forgers I've ever seen but you know they must have a release date pencilled in for you especially if you're saying you're going to go straight when you get out?"

"I dare say they have but the trouble is that I've been doing a bit of business in here like. Y'know day passes and such like."

"You're taking a bit of a chance forging them aren't you?"

"Well I know now don't I, but I thought it an easy enough way to make a few quid selling on the fags that I get paid for my work."

Denis said, "well, hopefully Charlie and me will be out in a few months' time."

"Oh, I know," said Pebbles, "Charlie's asked me to do a bit o'work for him, on the quiet like."

"What's that?" said Denis somewhat concerned.

Pebbles looked like he'd been caught out and said, "Oh nothing much, y'know, just a few bits and pieces," before he walked off rather sharpish.

Denis just looked at his disappearing back and wondered what Charlie was up to now.

Meanwhile Charlie had been giving one of the guards some back chat which had taken him out of the kitchens and landed him on toilet cleaning duties. It was only a bit of back chat cheek but the guard had had enough of him and so Charlie had the next few weeks cleaning all of the toilets much to his disgust. He was assisted by an ex-engineer who used to joke that the four inch diameter toilet out pipe was never designed for some of the prisoners who seemed to have developed six diameter arse-holes.

Denis thought he would play a trick on Charlie and found a roll of brown paper which he wet and shaped to look like an enormous turd. He then placed this, half on the seat and half in the toilet pan, in one of the cubicles shortly before Charlie was due to clean it.

They could hear the shout in the next prison block; "who the bloody hell has done this!" shrieked Charlie, "the dirty bastard as if they couldn't have at least got their aim straight!"

Denis and the others who were in on it laughed their socks off and Denis said, "I don't think Charlie is ever going to live that one down."

There were the occasional arguments between inmates mainly in respect of gambling which, although prohibited, went on anyway but other than that the time passed and before they knew it Denis and Charlie were up before the parole board.

Denis was considered to be an exemplary prisoner, with his time studying and working in the library and the board accepted his release date without question. The only reservation was in respect of where he would be living and so Denis said that he would be living at the Shelter and gave Tom's name and the Shelter address. He said that this where he intended to stay and that he would be living there during his parole.

For Charlie it was a bit touch and go as his run in with the guard had been recorded on his file. One member of the board questioned Charlie about this and the subsequent upset in one of the toilet cubicles. Charlie, for once exercised a bit of control and just shrugged it off saying that it was all a misunderstanding. The parole board found it difficult to keep straight faces as they were all aware of the practical joke played on Charlie with the brown paper. It was this that led them to grant his parole alongside Denis. Charlie had also given the Shelter as his contact details. Charlie was just glad to get out and didn't really care what lies he had to tell.

CHAPTER 40
Charlie and Denis back on the streets

They were released from prison at ten o'clock one morning in late November, just under the six months that they'd expected to serve. Both had picked up their belongings and they had enough for the bus fare back into town.

Neither had mobile phones or wallets and all they had were a few old keys and a bit of cash.

"What are those keys for Charlie, you know your house has long gone?" asked Denis.

Charlie said, "stick with me Denis and we'll be back in the high life before you know it."

Denis said, "now come on Charlie, you know we are both banned for at least five years from any financial trading activities in the broadest sense. We'll have to try and get proper jobs and also somewhere to stay. I think Tom will put us for tonight but then we'll have to move on. It looks like we're on the streets again."

"You might be on the streets but I'm not! You see this key here?" said Charlie holding up a small silver key.

Denis nodded with a puzzled look on his face.

Charlie went on, "this is the key to a security locker. It's like a post office box number where mail can be sent. I rented it for a couple of years quite a while ago now. Guess what's in it?"

Denis's eyes widened and said excitedly, "you don't mean you've got a stash of cash do you?"

"Shh.." said Charlie holding a finger up to the side of his nose. "That's exactly what I mean Denny boy, that's exactly what I mean. We'll go straight there and pick it up."

"Don't you think we should go to Tom's Shelter first in case anyone checks up on us?" asked Denis.

Charlie thought for a minute and said, "nah, I don't think they'll be bothered. They're just happy to get shot of us. I think we'll have to turn up and meet our parole officer as arranged but I don't think anyone will bother with us until then."

Denis said, "how much have you got Charlie?"

"I don't really know exactly, it's stuffed into envelopes inside this locker box."

Both Denis and Charlie were smiling by the time they got off the bus. They made their way over to the shop where the lockers were.

Inside the shop they nodded to the shop keeping who was standing behind his counter. An Asian man in his early thirties he asked, "can I help you."

Charlie just shook his head and said, "just come to pick up the post, that's all."

They made their way through the shop to the far wall where stood several rows of grey painted boxes about thirty centimetres square. There must have been at least two dozen and Denis said to Charlie, "which one's yours Charlie?"

"Can't you guess?" said Charlie, "unlucky for some, but lucky for others."

Denis said, "not number 13 surely?"

"Yep, got it in one, lucky 13 – well it is for me."

They approached the box and Charlie took out his key. Denis realised that he was holding his breath as Charlie fitted the key in the lock and turned.....

"What the F.....!" started Charlie as looked at the inside of an empty box.

They both went back to the shopkeeper and asked what had happened to box number 13. At first the shopkeeper didn't understand but then said that as no one had been into empty box 13 for several months no more mail could be placed in the box and so they opened it with the spare key they have and took out all of the mail and sent it on to the forwarding address.

"What f..f.. forwarding address is that?" asked a somewhat shocked Charlie.

"Why the one provided when the box was first rented," said the shopkeeper with a puzzled expression on his face. Crazy people he thought.

Denis and Charlie rushed out the shop confirming the shop-keepers opinion that they were crazy and looked for the bus stop that would take them back to the house that they had rented a couple of years ago when they had first got the money from the horse racing betting.

Denis said "didn't you think to change the forwarding address?"

"Several times," said Charlie, "but I just never got round to it!"

Charlie and Denis got round to the house they used to rent and knocked on the door. Initially there was no answer and so they knocked again much harder. Eventually a huge bloke came to the door in his vest and shorts. His arms and neck were covered in tattoos and there were several piercings about his face. He bellowed, "whadda ya want?"

Charlie began, "I'm Charlie Cooper and this is Denis Jackson. We used to live here a little while ago and believe some mail has been sent here and we've come to pick it up."

"No mail here for you here mate – you'd better move on," said the giant in a very menacing manner.

Denis said, "there must have been some letters for us. Cooper or Jackson? They're very important you see...."

"I've told you no letters, now piss off before I get angry!"

"But but…," stammered Denis.

"Do you like hospital food?" asked the giant as he towered over their heads.

Charlie and Denis stood their ground, after all there was quite a lot at stake here. But as neither of them wanted to tangle with this rough looking character they weren't sure what to do.

"Look, "began Charlie, "there could be something in it for you if you could just tell us if….."

"I won't tell you again, there's nothing here for you, now clear off!" and he turned and slammed the door in their faces.

Charlie and Denis turned to go and Denis whispered to Charlie, "how much was there Charlie?"

"I don't know exactly but there would have been tens of thousands of pounds if not hundreds of thousands."

Charlie continued, "there must be something we can do. Don't you know any 'muscle' Denis?"

Denis just shook his head and said that no he didn't tangle with anyone too prone to violence and said, "with all your crooked wheeling and dealing you must have come across some 'enforcers' sort of thing?"

"like you Denis I steered well clear of anyone who might want to take it out of me using force. I've always resorted to the law to resolve any differences," said Charlie rather ironically.

"Well the law can't help with this one can they?"

Charlie was almost crying as he was shaking his head in utter disbelief.

Denis looked physically sick as he said, "looks like it's back to Tom's then."

CHAPTER 41
Back on the streets

Tom welcomed them both back and said, "I must say I was most surprised when you wrote me saying that you had been in prison and needed somewhere to stay. What happened to all the money you both had?"

"Don't ask Tom," said Denis, "it's a long story."

Charlie looked aghast once more at the facilities and was on the verge of crying out loud when Tom said that in view of all their kindness in the past they could stay in the Shelter until they got straight provided it wasn't more than a few weeks, He felt it was the least he could after all the contributions they had made particularly over the previous couple of Christmases.

"Would we be able to stay over this Christmas Tom?" asked Denis.

"That might be pushing it a bit but let's see shall we," replied Tom. "You may be able to get on top of things by then and have jobs and somewhere to stay."

Just then Digger, Billy and Bert all showed up for something to eat. The last to shuffle in was Dobby Bobby who looked completely lost.

"Sorry to hear about Eddy, Bobby, Strin.... Denis told me," said Charlie. Eddy hadn't been well for some time and it had finally caught up with him. He passed away earlier in the year.

"Thanks Charlie, "said Bob, "it's life on the streets you know – it's a killer as you get older."

Denis and Charlie looked at each other both thinking well here we are back at square one. Talk about déjà vu they couldn't really believe that they had ended up exactly where they were a couple of years ago.

Denis said, "talk about a roller coaster ride, we've been up and down like a yo yo. I can't believe we went from rags to riches and back again in such a short space of time. We could have really done with that money Charlie."

Tom was looking at them both with a puzzled expression on his face and Denis said, "just ignore me Tom, put it down to the rantings of a mad man. I think I must had been mad not to have seen that things were likely to turn out this way."

Charlie just said, "well I've been rich and I've been poor but I think, as someone once said, I prefer being rich if only for financial reasons!"

The End